Sam, My Warrior

The Sam Ogden Mountain Man Series Vol. V

By Robert M. Johnson

Contents

First Publication October 21, 2015

By Creative Publications

(http//: Creative-Publications.com)

Robert M. Johnson PhD

Author and Publisher,

Palmyra, VA 22963

Introduction

The winter of 1826 finds young Sam Ogden living with the Mandan Indians in their village on the Missouri River. Life in the Slanted Village is built on the traditions of several hundred years. Sam and his mentor, Clyde Patterson have gradually become part of this complex network of practices and ceremonies. Sam has taken a wife, the daughter of Chief Rolling Thunder, her name is Little Fire.

In the few months that they have been married, the young couple have successfully made a home of their spacious mud hut on the prairie. The Slanted Village is comprised of more than fifty of these solidly built log and mud homes. But living so close to the great River, the Missouri, brings with it the danger of the white man's illness. Already, the Mandan have been decimated by these fierce epidemics and another is now upon them.

"Sam, my Warrior," is the fifth volume in the Sam Ogden Mountain Man Series. The story traces the evolution of the early Rocky Mountain West, marking its origins in the beaver trapping, fur trading period, through the gold rush phase and then into the cattle-raising period. The excitement of these simpler and nobler times continues to inspire us all! The series is as follows:

1. Hard to Kill
2. Winter Down
3. Rendezvous Prize
4. The Deerslayer's Destiny
5. "Sam, My Warrior"

Chapter 1: Hand to Hand

We had just come in from hunting antelope when the chief called me over to his hut. He said that a Blackfoot war chief had come that morning to the camp on a mission of vengeance. It appears that the man that I killed last summer at Feldman's trading post, Running Wolf, was his older brother and this man had come to avenge him.

The chief tried to make offerings of peace to the young warrior but it was no use. It was well known among the Blackfeet that I had made the kill shot on Running Wolf. The honor of the tribe required that his death be considered an insult and his brother was the one who must avenge what they considered a murder. I had told the chief how the attack had occurred and that Running Wolf had died a true warrior, charging at our men.

He told me that such was the account circulating around the villages of the frontier, but the Blackfeet could not accept such a story. They said Running Wolf was so great a warrior that killing him had to have been an act of cowardice on my part. "He says that you are a coward, hiding behind the 'great thunderstick,' so he called your rifle, my son," the chief replied.

I was holding the Hawken in my hands as he spoke and for just a minute, didn't understand what he was saying in the Mandan language. I quickly understood that I was being challenged to Hand To Hand combat by the Blackfoot warrior. It was about noon that day and all I could do was accept the challenge.

Clyde was with me and explained to me that I could use my hatchet and my knife in this kind of combat, but that was it. We walked back toward my hut and as we came close, Little Fire, my wife, came running to me, obviously frightened by what was happening. She was trembling as I held her close and at that moment the impact of the whole thing struck me like a club. I had never fought this kind of open battle with a trained adversary before!

This man I was facing had been doing this kind of rough and tumble fighting since he was a boy and all I had to show for my boyhood was lots of muscle from hard work on the farm. Clyde took me aside and explained that as a warrior I could not continue to show emotional attachment to my wife at this time, in front of the other members of the Mandan Tribe. They would see it as a sign of weakness. As I gathered my big hunting knife and my hatchet, he also said that the killing had to be done by knife or hatchet.

This kept getting more disturbing as it went along! I wanted to argue with my friend and mentor but the words seemed to freeze in my throat. He said there was another way to answer the challenge, it could be handled by using a pistol. That was going to be my next question, he answered it for me! So I tucked the pistol into my belt and mounted Challenger for the meet.

The prairie to the north of the Mandan Village was very level, and the ground was frozen now, with a light covering of snow. The horses would have good purchase as they ran at one another. This was a chance to test the mettle of my appaloosa, which, if Jacob Astor was correct, had been bred for this kind of mortal combat. Her breed had been conditioned from medieval times for battle service just like this was shaping up to be. Both of us would be sorely tested this day!

The hunt that morning had been uneventful, so Challenger was fit and ready for anything I would ask of her. We would see today if her bloodlines ran true.

Chapter 2: Eagle's Wing

As I rode out alone through the palisade gate, I could see immediately the shape of my enemy at a good distance across the field. Like his brother, he was riding an amazing war pony with large brown and black markings on a stark white coat. The horse seemed to be fighting his rider, as though he too was eager to attack, and he probably sensed I was riding a mare.

Now Challenger was beginning to show her own aggression, snorting and prancing as she liked to do when she became excited. We gradually came close to one another, the horses obviously agitated, almost bucking in their eagerness to engage in the fight. There it was again, the battle axe of the clan, the same one Running Wolf had, the one that was now a trophy at Feldman's Trading Post! This axe was painted red, and I could see the heavy triangular spike glistening in the noonday sun. It was surely a fearsome weapon.

The War Chief began shouting in his own language, and I could understand most of what he was saying as the Mandan and Blackfoot tongues share a common ancestry. "I am Eagle's Wing, brother of Running Wolf. I have come to kill you, coward!" He spit out these words as though the very thought of me filled him with disgust. He was pointing his long battle axe at me as he said it. My knife was in its sheaf at my side and I held my hatchet in my right hand, as I tried to control Challenger with my left.

Then, all hell broke loose, the horses both reared up and lunged at one another, their teeth bared in a fierce scream. When I saw the length of that battle axe, I was glad I had made a new longer handle of ash for my hatchet. It had become a small axe in the process, but matched his in size! As the horses rushed at one another, lashing out to bite, the Blackfoot and I became locked in a mutual effort to strike the head of our adversary with our two weapons brandished high in the air.

The horses were moving at full gallop when we met, but they were also nipping at each other through their bits. I have never felt anything so powerful as the meeting of our two battle axes in mid-air. The shafts broke and shattered, splintering into a dozen pieces and the two steel heads went flying out over the rumps of our horses!

We pulled the horses up, swinging them around to face one another again. But the Blackfoot had jumped to the ground with a short spear in one hand and a large hunting knife in the other. It was time for hand to hand combat, and he was ready to finish me off. I slipped from the saddle on the opposite side of my horse and he didn't see that I had pulled the pistol from my belt at the same time. My right arm was still stinging from the impact of the blow that shattered my hatchet, it smarted right up to the shoulder.

The Blackfoot expected to have the edge over me with his short spear, then he saw the pistol. The shock on his face was momentary, and he lunged with the spear pointed right at my chest. He expected to have the advantage with the sharp head of the spear and the length of its shaft. He was less than ten feet away when I pulled the trigger. The ball struck Eagle's Wing right below his jaw and ripped upward into his skull. It must have struck a large blood vessel because blood literally spurted from the entry wound in his throat, gushing down his buckskin shirt and he froze in mid stride.

I can't explain what happened next, he must have been already dead, but he continued to come toward me brandishing his spear, and lifting his knife in the air. I dropped the pistol which was now useless, and swung the hunting knife from my left hand over to my right, just in time to sink it into his belly and force it upward brushing the spear's advance aside with my elbow. Now I could hear the death rattle from somewhere deep in his throat, almost like a primal scream of death.

For just a moment we stood locked in this act of death and then his legs gave out and he crumpled down to the ground, bleeding profusely. It was over!

Chapter 3: DEATH RATTLE

I was so excited that things became a blur then. I just realized that Clyde and Little Hawk were standing there next to me, as we all looked down on what had been a very brave Blackfoot Warrior. Little Hawk bent down and with his knife removed the scalp lock of the dead man. He raised it high and let out a war cry that was jarring but truly expressed how I felt.

We both began to dance around the body of the dead warrior. There was so much pent up energy inside of me, I didn't know what else to do. Now the braves from the village were coming out and surrounding us, and the real war cries began in earnest. When the chief finally arrived, Little Hawk presented him with the scalp lock of Eagle's Wing.

The horse of Eagle's Wing was mine as a battle trophy. He stood off at a distance, his sides heaving still from the exertion, but too exhausted to run. I took his bridle and he looked in my eyes as his breath came in snorts and long gasps. It seemed as though we made a bond at that moment, he followed me without resistance as we headed back to the village.

At the palisade gate, I turned and looked out across the prairie where a small band of Blackfeet warriors sat their ponies on a rise across the river. They had come with their war chief to celebrate his victory of vengeance over the killer of his brother. Instead, they would tie his lifeless body over the back of one of their ponies and bear him back for burial.

I couldn't see their faces, but they were a grim reminder that the world of the frontier was an unforgiving and unforgetting place. For now, I was only going to enjoy this moment of victory, hard fought and hard won. The looks of those around me that afternoon, were looks of joy and celebration, and I was grateful that they understood that I only did what I had to do.

Clyde and Little Hawk took care of my horses for me. As I watched them lead Challenger away, I knew that we had passed the first real battle test together. She was as fierce as any horse I have ever seen, and she leaped into battle with a force and enthusiasm that did honor to her bloodlines. I felt a real pride in that horse!

Little Fire was there at the palisade entrance to hold me close and she could feel the intensity of my heart, which felt like it was going to burst. In her language, she whispered in my ear, "Tonight we will celebrate, Sam, my Warrior!" I couldn't see the smile on my face, but others told me later that it was one to remember.

There would be a tribal celebration that night, but the important celebration for me was walking at my side, Little Fire my wife. She would become my life that winter on the Missouri River. It was her duty as the wife of a warrior to check my body for scars and scratches, for wounds that I might have endured in the heat of battle. She told me that it was possible to come through an ordeal like hand-to-hand combat and have a wound you didn't even realize you had.

The mind becomes absorbed in the fierce fighting of the moment and everything else is forgotten while the body is forced to respond to the challenge to its survival. Thanks to the white man's pistol that I carried in my belt, I had no wounds from the spear or the knife of my adversary. He was certainly one who could've inflected very serious wounds if he had had the opportunity. Fighting with the white man's weapons was still new to the Indians though they were learning fast. The Blackfoot realized too late that he was overmatched and that the pistol I held in my hand would be his undoing.

The members of the Mandan Village never questioned my right to use the pistol in hand-to-hand combat. In their eyes my adversary had finally been killed by the stab wound of my hunting knife buried in his bowels and torn upward into his chest cavity and his heart. In the minds of those who mattered to me it had been a successful engagement of hand-to-hand combat and I had won. It was my first real individual combat situation though with time there would be many more. I was struggling to understand what it meant to be a warrior. Among the Mandan, my newly adopted family, that title was hard won and was measured in kills, like the one that had happened this afternoon.

Chapter 4: Parched Corn

When I got back to our hut, Little Fire had been making parched corn. It was our favorite food, and something that we shared together, both the work of it and the enjoyment. I loved the way the corn turned a darker color of red as it was slow cooked over a fire. We would then take and put it in a gourd with clear mountain water. We would let it settle until the water was sweetened by the corn and it made a wonderful drink, both satisfying and enjoyable.

She had prepared a little feast of parched corn for me as a reward for my efforts that day. I slowly chewed the corn as I looked into her eyes and she scanned my body for the wounds that every true Mandan wife was expected to find, if they existed. I was amused at how intent she seemed in her task running her hands over my skin and causing me to feel aroused by her tenderness and the warmth of her hands.

When she realized that there were no injuries then she became silly and started tickling me, causing me to jump and we both began to laugh. There was relief in the laughter as that afternoon our lives could've been changed forever had the outcome of the hand-to-hand combat been otherwise. We both knew that but it was unspoken between us and the laughter seemed to be our way of affirming the victory one more time. What Little Hawk, her brother, had done with his war cry and our little dance at the scene of the combat, was our way of expressing the relief of victory. Now, Little Fire and I were doing the same thing in the intimacy of our home.

Every time I thought of this being our home, it seems to me more and more meaningful. I felt like a rich man. I had a fine hut, almost a cabin, a beautiful wife who had made me the center of her life, I had everything a man could desire.

The price of what I had was clearly demonstrated by the conflict I had just gone through. I never thought life on the frontier was going to be easy, but I was naïve in thinking that you didn't have to pay a price for survival on the plains and on the frontier of the high mountains.

The fight that I just had with Running Wolf and now his brother Eagle's Wing, was clear evidence of the fact that just as the animals have their food chain with the larger animals holding all the place of power, so among humans there is a degree of power that comes from violence. It was up to me to adjust to that world, and thanks to those around me I felt that I was capable of dealing with whatever challenges came my way.

Every time you kill someone, no matter how justified the kill, you set in motion forces that could lead to more killing. The honor of the Blackfoot tribe had been injured by the death of their war chief, even though his behaviors and his tendencies toward others brought little honor to the tribe itself. It remained that their pride had been in injured by the fact that the whole war party had literally been wiped out.

Eagle's Wing was determined to make that right and he gave his life trying.

Chapter 5: Celebrate the Victory

As the long winter months continued to impose their restrictions on movement in the camp because of the cold, it seemed that the tribe found more reasons to celebrate. Clyde and I had smiled many times as we discussed the fact that it took almost nothing to bring the tribe together for a loud and friendly celebration. My hand-to-hand combat with Eagle's Wing, the fierce Blackfoot warrior, was certainly a cause for celebration that night.

Little Hawk and I and Clyde Patterson had been unsuccessful in our hunt for antelope that morning, but another party had brought in a large bull elk, and the hundreds of pounds of meat that animal provided would feed the tribe for several weeks. So that night we were celebrating my victory and also the killing of the bull elk!

As usual it was a time of feasting and dancing and chanting and much laughter. I was given a preferred place at the side of Chief Rolling Thunder. He gave a little speech to the warriors who sat around the circle, with the medicine man in his place of honor. He gave an account of my hand-to-hand combat with the Blackfoot warrior that afternoon. He held the scalp lock of Eagle's Wing high so all could see and the warriors all made sounds of approval and admiration. Some even broke out in little war cries, chanting over and over again their satisfaction that the Mandan were the strongest and bravest men on the Prairie.

I was beginning to have strange feelings of pride at moments like these because I felt part of something, after being someone who had no family and no home, I now was part of a family! The greatness of our family, that of Chief Rolling Thunder was contained in what each family called their Medicine Bag. The two Blackfeet scalp locks would now be part of the great medicine bag of our family! These men in whose company I was now an equal partner, were men that I could admire for their wisdom and their strength. I valued their courage in the face of obstacles that most city dwelling white men could never even imagine.

Living as close to nature as they did, facing the hardships that nature threw at them at every turn, through storms and snow and rain and fierce winds, these men and women lived a life of courage. What most white people would think of as heroic, among them was commonplace. I knew that with each one of these challenges that I was to face as a young warrior, my place among this group of men, Mandan Braves, would become more secure.

I was beginning to understand how men achieved greatness among a people who seemed externally impoverished. Their riches were much closer to nature than those of the white man. Having several horses, or even several wives, having a well-built hut, being a good hunter and harvesting fields of corn and other vegetables, that was the wealth of the Mandan Indian warrior and his family!

Their life was so completely dependent on nature that a bad year or a bad harvest would devastate their fragile economy of life. And yet they lived with a joy and enthusiasm that I could see every time I attended one of these amazing celebrations! Truly, they enjoyed being together. Just getting together had special meaning for the tribe, my family. It was indeed fascinating to listen, now that I could understand the language a little better, to their discussions and their decision-making which was always done in a communal manner.

My friend, Clyde Patterson, seemed to enjoy these life events as much as I did. I was very surprised at how emotional he had become when describing to me what the requirements were, regarding hand-to-hand combat that afternoon. He seemed to choke up as he spoke with me, and I thought he might even begin to tear up, he seemed so emotional. Perhaps better than I, Clyde understood the danger that I was in and he had seen the fierceness of warriors like Eagle's Wing.

But Clyde Patterson was learning to understand me as well. There were things about me that he would never know. Hidden in this youthful exterior was a fierceness and determination in my temperament that would one day make me an accomplished warrior. For now I felt giddy with the excitement of those around me and all I can remember about that night was that we laughed a lot, a lot.

Chapter 6: Mandan Winter

The celebration went on late into the night, until most of us were exhausted from dancing and chanting and telling stories. I was asked many times to recount the story of the death of Running Wolf and even more often the story of Eagle's Wing and the hand-to-hand combat of that afternoon. The people seem to have a gentle respect for what that kind of combat meant. They knew that it might've been very easy for me to either shun or deny the challenge and I'm not sure how they would've felt about me if I had.

I was beginning to feel as though I were accepted as a member of the village and the tribe even though I had hardly been there three months. It was a different feeling for me to be accepted in this way, almost unconditionally. It was still taking me a long time to feel that I belonged, that I could take advantage of the intense deep union here in this village as though I deserved to be a part of it.

I had known many different kinds of community in my life, from the hardscrabble farming community of Springfield Illinois to the boisterous and confusing community of mountain men at the trading posts and at the rendezvous. But this village, the Mandan Slanted Village as it was called, was a family experience of a whole different order. These people had been here for generations and hoped to be here for many generations more. Their greatest enemies seemed to be the white man's diseases which had already taken their toll on the Mandan nation of the Missouri Valley.

Clyde and I have been careful to stay within the village, having agreed that going out to the trading posts or to the Army posts would run the risk of bringing back some of the white man's diseases like measles and smallpox, pneumonia and the flu. The Indians lived a very close life in their village and we felt protective of them from this point of view.

When we finally went back to our hut that night, Little Fire and I were exhausted, both physically and emotionally. We made love that night but we both fell asleep almost immediately afterwards. Our closeness under the Buffalo robes was something that for the rest of my life will always be one of my fondest memories. Her generosity, from a physical perspective alone, was an act of love and beauty that I have never found equal anywhere, anyhow.

Ours was a privileged existence there in the quiet of our thick-walled mud hut. It felt as though we were far removed from all the turmoil and conflict of the world around us. When that world intruded on ours as it did that afternoon in the person of Eagle's Wing, we had to deal with it and then return to the comfort and quiet of our togetherness. I treasured those moments more than anything in the world.

I can't say that I lived for conflict and for the moment of battle but I also realized the excitement and gratification that came from acquitting oneself against other men of equal or even greater force. I know that some men relish the life of the warrior and seem to thrive on the emotional high that comes from killing another human being. Maybe I just haven't done enough of it yet at this stage in my life, but killing brings me little or no satisfaction.

My fight with Eagle's Wing that day had been an act of necessity. If I had not gone out to meet him he would've come in to get me and I'm not sure what would've happened then. He would've placed my tribe, the Mandan, and my wife at great danger. I did what I had to do and now it's over. For now.

Chapter 7: Husking Corn

This year had been an especially successful year for the crops at the Mandan Village. The rain and sunlight had been exceptional and the corn crop had come in more abundant than usual. I was informed by my Mandan wife that her family's corn was among the best in the village. I wondered what she meant by that until I finally got the explanation I was looking for.

For the Mandan, the cultivation of crops is done by the women and the men cultivate only tobacco for their own use. For generations, the women have been managing their garden plots with consistent success, from season to season. According to Little Fire, each family had its own particular type of corn that they raised, its seeds being passed from one generation of women to the next. As I looked at the cache of vegetables that we kept in our living quarters, I was impressed with the corn that we had taken in. The ears were stripped of their natural green covering but they were heavy and long and seemed extremely healthy.

The corn had been left for several months to dry, and now it was ready to be stripped down. Some of the husks would be used for fodder for the animals, especially the horses and goats during the wintertime. The kernels of corn would be stripped from the cobs and the dry cobs would be used for the fires in the winter. The Indians seemed to have perfected the complete use of whatever they grew or hunted. If they grew squash, after using the pulp for their food and even making breads of the soft pulp, they would dry the outer shell and use it to carry water or as a canteen for the trail.

The sunflowers that they grew would be used as part of their pemmican. Beaten to a pulp, the seeds would be included along with dried venison and berries in this amazing food that seemed to last so long and keep so well, especially on the trail. The dry shells of the sunflower seeds would be used for fire starting and when they were dried sufficiently, they seem to ignite without any effort.

This was the life I was being introduced into by my Mandan wife. The work in the village was carefully determined ahead of time. With the women doing certain tasks while the men were expected to uphold the honorable vocation of warrior and hunter. There were religious ceremonies for just about everything that was done within the village, from erecting a hut to planting corn, to going on a hunt. It was the role of the medicine man to make sure that all of these religious ceremonies were accomplished as required by long-standing tradition.

The favor of the spirit world was sought for every adventure and every important task in the life of the Indians. I did my best to keep up with all these various superstitions, though I have to admit that my confidence in the spirit world was never that strong. My wife seemed to believe wholeheartedly, as did her brother Little Hawk, and that was good enough for me. I think the Indians were expecting me to be more resistant to this aspect of their life, but when I wasn't, they took it in stride. It was something they had always believed in, that was just the way it was.

But Little Hawk and I were becoming concerned about the fact that the elk meat that had been brought in by the other hunting party was rapidly disappearing even though it was a large supply of meat. He told me that he knew of a place where we could get a moose if we were willing to ride far enough toward the distant hills. Clyde Patterson and I were always willing to take on a project of that importance, as we felt that we were just taking advantage of our situation with the Mandan, their food supplies were so abundant. Clyde and I knew that we would be able to contribute more substantially to the life of the tribe if we could do one of our moose hunts.

When we heard that Little Hawk had a hunting expedition in mind for the pursuit of moose, Clyde and I knew that we would be joining that expedition for certain. After three months at the Mandan Village I was beginning to feel a bit of what we had jokingly called at our previous winter living quarters, "cabin fever." I was ready for a good long ride.

Chapter 8: Moose Hunt

We saddled up early that next morning and, taking plenty of supplies for a long trip, we set out in a westerly direction heading toward a small range of mountains that jutted out from the eastern side of the Rockies. We knew it would be a good two or three days ride just to get to the foothills where we would be hunting. We were in the heart of winter but the prairies were kept fairly clear because of the blowing wind. The snow seemed to gather along certain natural lines of the terrain. The slight rises, little hills, riverbanks, gullies, all seemed to be gathering places for the winter snows of the prairies.

I found it amazing how the Indians knew how to ride this rugged country. They knew that the snow seemed to stack up at certain rises and along certain riverbanks, so they rode accordingly. I watched with cautious amazement as Little Hawk and several of his fellow warriors led us along a trail that seemed to appear out of nowhere. There was just enough snow covering the ground to make it hard to see, but they seemed to just know it was there. We never deviated in the slightest from our direct westerly route.

The bright sun that morning made everything seem whiter than white. The brilliance of the countryside caused the sun's light to bounce off shrubs and sagebrush, trees and riverbeds. There was a moment of magic as the sun cascaded over the prairie that morning and I felt as though my heavy coat was soaking in the warmth of that early morning. It was good to be alive.

We camped that first night in a copse of cottonwoods along a river bank. We had to break the ice to get to the clear water running along the rocky bed of the little river. Damn, that water was cold! I still remember it like it was yesterday.

There had been no sighting of riders at all that day so we made a fire that evening and its heat was welcome after a cold day in the saddle. Little Hawk explained to me that on the prairie, because it was so open, they were not able to create what he called way stations, or travel huts. He said that they would be using one or two of those in the mountains when we reached that area. These were rough structures that were left from season to season, from year to year, for hunting parties or war parties to move about in the rough wilderness.

He said that often they were just a gathering of poles that formed the leaning roof for shelter against the elements. They made it easier to set up a quick shelter, especially if the weather was bad. He said all the men in his village were trained to quickly establish shelter when they encountered a difficult situation like sleet or snow, especially blizzard conditions. He told me that they could have a shelter set up for protection in the blink of an eye and he snapped his finger to show me what he meant.

These were traditions that went back as far as the arrival of his people in the land of the mountains and the prairie. They had learned to adapt and adjust, and from generation to generation these skills have been passed down because hunting was their way of life. They depended on it to survive through the winter. I'm sure my amazement showed in my face when he explained this to me, it made so much sense!

Clyde and I discussed this tactic of hunting as we sat with our pipes around the fire that night. The other Braves had already gone to sleep and you could hear light snoring from our party of seven. It was rare now that Clyde and I had time to talk together like this, since I was spending most of my time with my new bride. There was a lot to catch up on and we talked late into the night, probably much later than we should have as sunrise came early that next morning.

We had made our beds at night with cottonwood branches stripped from the trees surrounding our Little River encampment. Two good heavy buffalo robes beneath me and I was good for the whole night, it's amazing how those heavy skins could keep out the cold!

Chapter 9: Mountains Again

By the third day we were approaching the little mountains that led up to the Rockies in the distance. We were probably a good five to ten miles from the Rockies themselves but the small mountains provided plenty of cover as they were densely forested. I could see why the Indians had found this moose wallow. This pre-range of mountains as I would call it, extended a good twenty miles north to south along the eastern range of the Rockies.

I would estimate their height at about 4 to 5000 feet up from the prairie, which itself might have been at two or 3000 feet of altitude already. By Rocky Mountain standards that was not very high, and the trees that covered this small range of mountains were mostly pine with some aspens and maples spread in among them. We found a streambed that was pretty dry and had only a small amount of ice down its main center. It was wide enough for us to walk our horses upward for about 2000 feet.

Little Hawk assured me that the streambed lead directly to a small canyon where the moose loved to hole up for the winter. From my past experience of hunting moose in the winter I knew that they sought out these small canyons because of two important weather factors. The canyon provided security and safety from wind and from snow. It always amazed me how the sheltered canyons could be literally almost green with vegetation while all around there might be several feet of snow on the ground.

But there was another factor that the moose utilized the canyon for. And that was to prevent attacks by predators like grizzly bear or mountain lions or most dangerous of all, a wolfpack. The moose is a different kind of animal than an antelope or even an elk. Deer, elk or antelope when confronted with a predator like a grizzly bear or a wolf or even a cougar, would try to out run the predator. Because of its physical makeup, the moose was not that good at endurance running. Don't get me wrong, the moose can move very fast when it wants to!

The fact of the matter is that the moose can only move that fast for very short distances. Where an antelope might run for five or ten miles at a stretch, the moose is only good for probably about a tenth of that. That puts the moose in a lethal danger from its predators, because after trying to out run the predator, the moose is obviously in dire physical straits from exhaustion and more vulnerable than ever to the attack.

I've seen a pack of wolves run down a full-grown moose and once the prey is completely exhausted, they just leap up on it, pulling it down to the ground and the huge animal has no energy left to fight. A small family of moose will depend on the antlers of the bull to defend them when attacked by large predators like grizzly bears, wolves or mountain lions. The female, not having that set of antlers and its dangerous power, must rely on her hooves for survival and protection. The force of those hooves is amazing though!

On one occasion I saw a female moose defending her calf against several wolves. With one single kick from a powerful hind hoof, she broke the back of a full-grown wolf!

It was one of the most amazing survival things I've ever seen in the wild and I can still remember it to this day. The painful sound that wolf made when it's back snapped from the kick of the big moose, was gut wrenching. The cow and her calf ran away that day, escaping from the wolves which were undermanned, I guess you'd say. A small pack of three wolves is not a match for a full-grown moose, it takes more like five or ten to take down that big an animal.

I went down into the little Valley that day and put that poor wolf out of his misery, also got a great pelt out of that one, I must admit. Didn't have to shoot it bring it down, I just cut its throat and then skinned it out. Left the entrails and the carcass for the other wolves who came back after a few hours and found no compunction in eating what was left of their own pack member. Some things are hard to understand about wild animals, but that's what makes them wild.

Chapter 10: Moose Wallow

As expected, the little streambed that we were following led to a much larger opening in the side of the small mountain. We were up at about 5000 feet I would estimate, and a canyon opened before us, reaching high toward the summit of the little mountain. There we could see what amounted to a waterfall though it was mostly frozen up there in the middle of winter. The falling water made amazing sculptures of ice that framed what was left of the waterfall that seeped down through from above. With the sun shining on it that day, the ice became like crystals of light radiating a natural beauty that's hard to describe.

The canyon led back several miles into the heart of the mountains and there was almost like an elbow leading back even further. We sat our horses there and Little Hawk explained to me that this particular canyon went back a long way into the side of the mountain. He said there was even a cave back there at the far end. For our purposes, this narrow opening in the mountain served as a winter quarters for a large family of moose. It was a favorite hunting spot for the Mandan and from what we could tell by the tracks in the snow, this year would be a good hunt!

By the time we reached that spot at the front edge of the canyon, it was already getting dark and we found one of the Mandan shelters there. As Little Hawk had explained to me, the shelter was really just a pile of poles and heavy branches that formed a kind of lean to against the side of the canyon. A large rock jutted out from the edge of the canyon wall and the Indians had simply placed some heavy tree trunks and long branches against the opening.

The men seemed to know exactly what to do and soon they were stripping branches from pine trees to place over the heavy poles that formed the roof of the shelter. In no time at all the shelter was covered with an opening for a cook fire in the roof between the logs. It was large enough to easily accommodate the seven of us with the fire pit in the middle. In no time at all a fire had been made and each of the Braves was taking his place around the fire. The floor of the lean to was already covered in pine branches so all we had to do was put down our Buffalo robes and we were ready for the night!

We cooked a stew of buffalo meat that we had brought with us, that had been dried and smoked from the Buffalo hunt earlier that year. Cornmeal and ground sunflower seeds had been thrown in to thicken the stew and a turnip or two had been added. We enjoyed the hearty meal that night around the warmth of the fire as each one sat huddled in a buffalo robe against the cold. I never realized how important wind was when it came to a cold winter night. I learned that lesson that cold night of the moose hunt.

We were so far down into the protective gully of the canyon that no wind moved at all along that sheltered space. We could hear the wind moving across the mountainside above, but it was ten feet above us and we were sheltered and protected within the walls of the canyon. Our horses had been gathered together in a small natural corral not too far from our encampment and I could see that the Mandan had been using this location for many generations because everything seemed to be perfectly setup.

There was running water from the stream coming off the side of the mountain and trickling through the walls of ice that surrounded it. There were little pools of water for the horses to drink and plenty of cold freshwater for the men. Pulling together two or three fallen pine logs was all that was needed to finalize the small corral for the horses and the two pack horses we had brought along to carry meat back with us. Little Hawk had suggested that I bring Horace along as he had become attached to my horse, Challenger anyway.

Anytime I took Challenger out by herself without Horace, things got messy in the Mandan herd. The Indians said that Horace would throw a temper tantrum, braying and honking almost in his frustration at being without his friend and companion, Challenger! Horace always continued to be a mystery for me, but I had long forgotten my anger at him for his cantankerous ways. Here on the trail of the moose, Horace and Challenger and I made kind of a team, I thought. Clyde loved to tease me about that, knowing the history that I had with that God damn mule!

Chapter 11: Sunrise Hunting

Little Hawk had told me that we would be up well before sunrise that next morning because he said the moose love to move about in the early hours at daybreak. We wanted to be there when they began foraging about for what food they could find that day in the little canyon that was their winter quarters. The horses would stay in their corral there at the campsite and one of the Braves was assigned to stay there with them for protection and to bring up the pack horses once the killing started.

Our party expected to take at least three moose during this expedition and the two pack animals would have to carry back the meat. Besides that, each one of the riders would carry a sack of at least twenty or thirty pounds of meat for their families. We were up early that morning and had a quick breakfast of pemmican and cornmeal. I'd come to love chewing on the parched corn that we made, as it was very satisfying to eat and the taste was excellent.

We each took a small gourd of Springwater with us for the journey that day. We could not calculate how long we would be out as the canyon stretched back several miles and we would follow it as far as we needed to. Six of us proceeded on foot, following the canyon bed in the faint light of the moon, which soon gave way to the first gray light of the new day. Clyde and I had our rifles and each had a pistol in our belt as well. Little Hawk was also carrying a rifle, which he knew how to handle with expertise.

The other three braves carried spears and bows with full quivers of arrows. Each of us carried a sharp hunting knife that we would use for the skinning when it came time for that. We moved as quietly as we could, knowing that sounds were magnified against the walls of the large canyon. We made our way through clusters of heavy rocks that we were able to manage because of our heavy winter boots.

The air in the canyon was so heavy that after a while I could begin to smell the moose, to my surprise. This was a new experience for me, knowing that animals like deer and moose and just about every predator in the wilderness depended on smell for survival. I was having the same experience that the animals would have. Which made me realize of course, that the moose could smell me coming up into their territory as well!

The sun began to cast a brighter light now as we approached what was specifically the moose location, what we hunters called the moose wallow. It was a place where the moose bedded down for the night and where they spent most of their time in the safety and security of their hideaway. It usually consisted of a small stand of trees which could be anything from jackpines to cottonwoods, to willows or aspens. They liked it thick and near a water source.

Now we could hear them moving about, their hooves making clacking sounds along the rocks that echoed off the walls of the canyon. They were probably grazing at that time already this early in the morning. I was surprised at the amount of vegetation in the small canyon, there were still a lot of grasses and small shrubs that obviously were being eaten by the moose this far into the winter. There probably wasn't much nutrition or nourishment in what they were eating but the roughage was enough to keep their bellies full.

As the sun now cast a much brighter light around the walls of the canyon we could begin to see shapes and outlines of the large animals and I was really surprised to see almost a dozen of them spread out over the far end of the canyon. The canyon opened up into in large arena, almost a mile across and there the moose were feeding. Occasionally one would raise an antlered head and look around as though sniffing and checking the air for intruders.

We kept our selves hidden under cover of trees and rocks and took our time to estimate what would be the best kill shots for us among this large number of moose. I did not expect to see this many in one place at one time. Moose tend to be more of a solitary animal, not a herd animal.

Chapter 12: Killing Field

As we watched these large animals feeding in the haze of that early morning, I realized that soon the tranquility and peacefulness that we were witnessing would be turned into a killing field. Life on the frontier and in the wilderness was that way. We could have been a grizzly bear, a cougar, or a pack of wolves, and each predator would be doing the same thing we were doing at that moment. Creeping closer and closer to our prey and making sure that we would take our best shot.

Little Hawk was giving arm and hand signals now to the others to spread out and allow an access place for the animals to pass by. We were all aware that these large animals had nowhere to go away from us. They could not run in the only direction that would provide safety because the walls of the canyon held them confined. What they would do, is they would turn toward us and run at us, to escape down in the direction of the canyon from which we had come. There were many side avenues where they could find shelter once they passed us at the edge of the large opening there at the end of the canyon.

Little Hawk explained to me the night before that the strategy would be for us to shoot at least three of the large animals while they were standing and grazing in place. Then we would attempt to take one coming at us on the run. We would stay behind whatever shelter we could find whether it was tree or rock and hope to kill one animal coming through the opening that we created. He had explained to us what we were about to do the night before seated around the campfire. But he also pointed out the one point of danger, which was that we would be shooting across a short distance but shooting right at one another!

We had been reminded to be careful of this and that any shot taken must be taken before the animals crossed the invisible line that we had created at the edge of the canyon opening. There was only one way for the moose to travel and we were to be careful not to kill any young moose only take mature animals either cows or bulls. It was decided that Little Hawk would take the first shot and that once his gun went off, all hell would break loose.

The booming of his rifle coincided with one of the closer animals falling to his knees and making a very pitiful wailing sound almost like that of a pig being slaughtered. Clyde and I opened up immediately shooting at a large bull together with the hopes of bringing him down quickly with our two shots. That effectively did happen, and the three braves with the bows and arrows were also focused on a female moose that was close to them.

We were reloading as fast as we could but at that moment, in that split-second, the moose began running in utter chaos. Their instincts had told them that they were safe in this remote valley from predators and so when panic took over, they had no idea what to do next, they had no plan. As a result they ran at each other, ran against the far wall of the canyon and finally after much loud snorting and kicking at one another as though they were their own enemy, the whole group of eight moose began a concerted run, they stampeded for the entrance of the canyon, right where we stood.

Clyde and I were reloaded now as was Little Hawk and so as the moose began their attack on our position, just as we expected they would, we leveled in on an animal that we agreed on, Clyde and myself. It was a young bull who was moving at a good speed and coming right at us giving us very little target so we had to shoot for the front of his chest.

Our musket balls struck both at the same time right in the very center of the young bull's chest as he came toward us. His front legs collapsed, causing him to drop his young antlered head to the ground as he slid forward. I saw his tongue come out and I heard a strange gasping sound come from his throat as he hit the ground just ten feet in front of us. The bows of the three warriors seemed to have little effect at that point and Little Hawk himself had not made the third kill. As it turned out, four moose were down, and the eight others were now long gone down the canyon. We all let out a whoop of excitement over our great hunt!

Chapter 13: Harvest the Kills

Four animals were down, and my God, they were big!
Two of them were not dead yet and were flailing about with
their hooves kicking in all directions. Hunters had to be very
careful at a time like this because those sharp hooves could
be lethal if you didn't approach the animal properly.
Everyone knew that it was foolish to try to kill a downed
moose with arrows, you might shoot a half a dozen times to
kill it, even if you were lucky.

A man with the rifle was reluctant to use another shell
to kill an animal in its death throes. The easiest way to handle
the situation was to take out your hunting knife and approach
the animal from behind its back, above his head, especially if
it was antlered, and slit the animal's throat with your hunting
knife. Nothing would be more messy than that though, as
once the blood started to flow it seemed to come out in
gallons. But we had two animals down who were not dead
and we had no choice except to take out our knives to finish
the job.

The Indians were whooping and jumping up and
down and they were so excited about the success of our kill
that they were not about to do the final honors on the two
writhing, flailing, snorting, enraged animals on the ground.
That left Clyde and myself to do the dirty work and we did as
we had to, trying our best to hold the head of the animal

down kneeling on its neck and slitting his throat from side to side. The blood that came gushing out was obscene, but it was the only way to put the animal out of its misery. Now Little Hawk was organizing the skinning and butchering of the animals and he took a strange horn from his pack that he carried, and blew twice on the horn.

The horn looked like it had been made from a buffalo's horn and the sound echoed through the valley which had become ominously silent now. The sound reverberated through the canyon walls and I realized right away what he had done. He had signaled to our fellow hunter, who was managing the horses, to bring up the two pack horses for loading with the meat that we would be taking from the carcasses.

It was still early morning when we began the butchering and skinning process and to my surprise the heavy winter furs of the moose were magnificent and thick. They would be great protection against the cold of the long winter months ahead. To make things go faster we decided to work in teams of two and we had four animals down. Clyde and I began working on the large moose that we had killed with our first shots and soon we were pulling back the hide from his hindquarters. You could hear that strange ripping sound again of an animal, a large animal being skinned.

It always amazes me the amount of entrails that you got from an animal like this and we dumped them on the ground so that it would be easier to move the body back and forth when we had to finish our skinning and butchering. Taking out the intestines and the bowels and the heavier organs of heart and liver for a large animal like this was a messy process but one that had to be done immediately in order to complete the skinning of the carcass. We worked as fast as we could and had finally removed all the skin from the first large animal and were beginning on the second when we heard something we didn't want to hear it all, a loud howl! Wolves!

Little Hawk looked up from what he was doing with one of the moose cows and said only one word in Mandan, "Faster!" He knew we now had to work much faster in order to get the job done before the wolves became a factor. We did not want to have to spend half of our manpower fighting off wolves while we continued to work at the butchering of these magnificent animals we had killed.

We'd spoken the night before about the possibility of wolves following our trail as they would act as though they were scavengers picking up after our kill. In fact we would be obliged to leave them the entrails of these large animals, especially if we had to hurry to leave the killing field. We would prefer to take the heart and liver of the moose with us but that would mean more butchering and more careful exploration of the entrails. For now, we wanted muscle meat and hide and we would be willing to leave the rest to the wolf pack. The howls were now becoming louder and more frequent, meaning a large wolf pack was descending upon us.

Chapter 14: Large Wolf Pack!

Because they were more agile and closer to the ground, the wolves could descend along the walls of the canyon at certain spots where the horses or moose could not pass. Obviously, this Wolfpack knew their way around and they were coming down one of those chutes. Now we had a twofold problem on our hands. We had a killing field that was covered with blood and giving off the strong scent of good meat to a Wolfpack that was probably hungry from a long winter of scarce hunting.

But the other and equally important factor in our situation was the horses we had corralled lower in the canyon. Wolves had learned that the way humans kept horses and even mules was a boon to their hunting efforts. The amount of effort that it took a wolf to put down a horse, a wild stallion for instance, in the wilderness, made it almost prohibitive for a Wolfpack to chase after an animal that could move with that speed across that distance.

What humans were doing for wolves was corralling horses and keeping them under control in a corral or even hobbled, so all a pack of wolves had to do was slither into a corral and they had the horses captive right there! The horses couldn't run move, they could barely fight because there was so little space. I've heard stories where a wolf jumped on the back of a horse and with his powerful jaws bit into the neck of the horse, causing the poor animal to panic so that the other wolves could easily gain access to its haunches and its throat from underneath.

For someone who kept horses as I did, and depended on them as I did, the thought of a horse dying in such a frightful manner sent shivers up and down my spine. We were about a mile out on foot from our horse corral and the wolves were descending into the canyon. Our Mandan crew had to make a decision immediately. The sound of the wolves howling made it clear that they were already descending into the canyon.

I had to think fast at that moment because I was very concerned about my horse and my mule back at the corral and Little Hawk could understand my apprehension. I spoke to him in rapid English saying that Clyde and I would go back to defend the corral and do what we could to stop the Wolfpack from advancing on either a killing field or on our horse corral. He agreed with me that that was the best alternative for the time being and they would continue to butcher there at the hunt site.

As we began to move toward the trail that led down the canyon, we could see the Indian brave who had been in charge of the horses leading Horace and the other pack horse up toward the killing field. We knew now that there was no one to defend the horse corral and so we had to hurry to get back in time before the wolves decided they wanted a meal of horse flesh.

Clyde and I had already reloaded our muskets so we were ready and each of us had a pistol with a double shot in it. That would give us some leverage against the Wolfpack, depending on how big it was. Wolf packs had been known to number as many as ten and sometimes as many as fifteen or twenty wolves during the harsh killing season of the winter.

We set off at a trot heading down the trail as fast as we could, trying to make sure of our footing because the rocky terrain made it easy to twist an ankle or break a leg. Because we were going downhill we made the mile distance in probably about a quarter of an hour. Our timing was perfect. The wolves had just begun to gather around the corral where the horses were being kept. I always thought that if I was a wolf, having horses in a trap like that would be like Christmas and all the holidays rolled up into one. What a gift!

As we were expecting, there were about a dozen wolves spread out all around the corral. Some of them were hiding in the rocks, some of them snarling at the horses, their fangs bared and growls coming from deep within their throats. It was our good fortune that the wolves had not figured out what their strategy was going to be by the time we got there. They knew instinctively that horses' hooves were dangerous and that seven horses confined like that would put up a hell of a fight. They had just figured out what they were going to do by the time we got there. Damn, these were big wolves!

Chapter 15: Kill the Alpha

A Wolfpack, as I had learned from my mentor Clyde Patterson, is a highly structured social reality. Two members make up the key to the hierarchy: the alpha male and the alpha female. They were the ones in charge of planning the strategy for taking down this herd of horses that they had before them. Seven horses in a corral was a godsend for a Wolfpack and would provide them with food for weeks on end. And these horses were trapped.

Clyde and I found cover behind a fallen tree and the trunk provided us with a good resting place for our muskets as we began firing. At first, it was hard to pick out the alpha male and the alpha female, though usually they were the larger animals in a pack. So we began firing at will, taking out as many wolves as we could. We were shooting at least one shot every thirty seconds and that went on for probably several minutes. There were five wolves down by the time we finished shooting.

The others had now disappeared into the underbrush and over the rocks. Several of the wolves that were down were not dead and they were howling and grunting and snorting in their rage and pain. We could barely see the other wolves but we knew they hadn't gone very far, they were regrouping somewhere behind the rocks of the canyon.

We approached the dying wolves, there were three of them still live and they were lying on the ground with their legs flailing as though they were running from an enemy. You could see the fear in their eyes, in a matter of seconds they had been turned into prey! That was not the way it was supposed to be, nature had put them in charge, they were at the top of the food chain! But now here they were lying in pain, suffering on the ground and bleeding, bleeding.

Again, to not waste ammunition on a dying animal, we used our hunting knives to slit the throats of the wolves and we realized that at least one of the wolves we killed, had to be the alpha male. God he was a big animal for a wolf. I had heard fantasy stories of dire wolves and wondered if he might almost qualify, he was so damn big. We dragged the bodies over to the side and stacked them out of sight of the corral around behind a pile of large rocks. Wolves, even dead ones, made horses frantic.

We had to try to calm the horses down because otherwise they would've kicked down the fragile corral we had built for them and they would be long gone, you can be sure of that. The eyes of a horse when they are in utter panic are amazing! They are so expressive of the fear and anguish that survival has built into them, that it makes you feel sorry for them that they cannot even understand when they are no longer in danger.

We humans knew that the situation was under control and the wolves presented no further danger to our animals there in the corral. That was fine to say, but for the horses they didn't know what we knew and all they could smell was the acrid smell of Wolf everywhere, dead ones and live ones!

Clyde and I were caught in a quandary at that point, not knowing what to do to calm the horses down because they were about to kick their corral to pieces and head off at full gallop across the prairies below. We would've been in a sorry situation if we hadn't come up at that time and stopped the wolf attack. I estimate that we had probably covered almost a hundred miles from the Mandan Village and to walk all that way back in the winter, especially with all that meat, and if there ever was a blizzard on the prairies, we could all die in short order.

One of the horses in particular seemed to be in a state of complete and utter chaotic panic. Clyde ducked into the corral and with his bandanna covered the face of the horse while he stood alongside of it and talked to it in a soothing way and rubbed its flanks with both hands. Now that the horse couldn't see anything and its sense of smell was completely overwhelmed by the scent of Clyde sensed through the bandanna, the horse calmed down instantly. The effect of that was that each horse felt the same general calm, it was like a ripple effect through the small herd of seven horses and soon they had all calmed down.

My horse, Challenger, was the last of them to really finally give up the frenzy. She had been running back and forth across the length of the corral and I was almost expecting her to leap over the corral which was almost five feet high. I always thought she had it in her to do that, but once she saw Clyde come into the corral, she seemed to accept his presence and slowed down in her frenetic racing back and forth.

Chapter 16: Finish the Job

While this battle was going on with the Wolfpack down below, the five Indians were working at a fever pitch to finish the butchering of the moose at the killing field. They had loaded the meat from two of the moose on to the packs already and one of the Indians was beginning to lead the pack horse back down toward the corral, in the hopes of providing some support of our effort against the Wolfpack.

It was just our luck that the Wolfpack had chosen to go after the horses instead of going for the easy kill up at the moose carcasses. The horse corral was a distraction that worked to our advantage. The wolves probably sensed the presence of human predators and felt that they were about to have an easy situation with the horses we had abandoned there in the corral. Clyde and I arrived on the scene just in time to interrupt their grand scheme.

We could hear now the pack horse coming down, picking his way slowly along the rock filled stream bed where we had just walked ourselves. I went up to meet the Mandan brave who was coming down with the pack horse, while Clyde began skinning out the wolves that we had killed. Those wolf pelts would be worth some serious money at the next rendezvous, we both knew that. Five wolf pelts would bring almost a hundred dollars and would make our venture with Little Hawk more than worth our while!

The pack horse was clearly overloaded and that's why he was picking his way with such care, instinctively knowing that anytime he would slip on the rocks of the streambed that the weight of the pack would take him down. The young Mandan was being very careful and rightly so to make sure that he got his charge down to the base camp where he knew we would be waiting for him.

We had brought with us several gunny sacks of burlap that we expected to be able to use to carry the moose meat on our journey back. The three of us began filling those sacks now and soon we had three sacks filled and that lightened the load on the pack horse to something that he could handle going all the way back to the Mandan Village.

The young brave, a young man named River Otter, was amazed at the wolves we had killed and between the three of us we had them skinned out in no time at all. Now we could hear the others coming back down the trail leading Horace, who every once in a while let out a resistive bray letting everyone know he was a reluctant participant in this foolishness. I walked up the path about a half a mile to meet them so that I could help them get Horace to cooperate.

As always, I had a couple of cubes of turnip hidden in my pocket and Horace knew that. As soon as he saw me he looked up and began walking toward me on his own. Little Hawk and the other Indians just stood back and watched the scene as Horace came toward me and nudged my jacket pocket, instinctively knowing exactly where the turnip cubes were. I held one out for him, one which I'd taken out of my pocket earlier and he gobbled it down smacking with his lips and grunting in a satisfied manner. He then let out a soft fart and let me lead him down the trail without any resistance. The other Indians just laughed, they thought it was funny because the poor animal was loaded with moose meat, he was carrying several hundred pounds.

I always admired the stamina of these big mules like Horace, once you got past the temperament, they were quite an amazing animal. They could haul loads of several hundred pounds and do it on the most difficult and unstable terrain. They seemed to have no fear of heights, but you did have to feed them properly, a mule couldn't be fed like oxen. Oxen just didn't care what the hell they ate as long as they could eat something, dry grass or hay didn't make any difference to them. Mules, you had to feed in a more reasonable manner, they needed occasional oats and good hay to keep them going.

Then as I also had learned, some of them because of their nasty personalities need to be fed turnips on a regular basis. I was never sure whether this meant that he was smarter than other mules, or just more ornery! But that was how Horace and I developed our sterling relationship!

Chapter 17: Getting Gone

Little Hawk assessed the situation at the corral and checked to see that the horses were all okay and then looked with amazement at the five wolf pelts that we had harvested there at the corral. He smiled in recognition of our accomplishment and then said to me, "I believe we should move out right away!"

It was still mid to late afternoon and we knew that we could probably make it down to the prairie at least and out of the canyon by nightfall. That would give us some distance from the wolves and we could hear occasional howls along the mountainside, indicating that they were still around and still presented a danger.

Every time a wolf would howl from the mountainside the horses would pick up their ears and we knew that they were not going to tolerate being around wolves very long. Horses did have a will of their own and when panic took over, you simply had to get out of the way because they were going to run and run like hell. We couldn't afford to take that chance and so it was the right decision for us to leave the canyon and the Valley and get back down to the prairie where we knew there was another waystation set up by the Mandan hunting parties.

We made good time getting down to that waystation and as usual the men put the shelter together in quick order and got the horses well set in a makeshift corral. We took the pack racks off the two pack courses that is to say Horace and the other pack horse, and placed the racks with the moose meat close to the fire where they would be safe from predators who might be lurking around the fringes of our camp.

We had a good meal that night of moose steak, and damn, that fresh meat cooked up good! The men were all in good spirits and we had plenty of water that we carried down from the upper spring so we had a good meal that night, and it made up for the heavy work that we'd done that day. The meat we had harvested came at quite a price of effort, but we were glad to have paid the price and accomplished such a successful hunt. We all slept well that night though we took turns guarding the horses and the meat.

We were up early the next morning and back on the trail heading home now at a good pace. I don't know what it is about horses and travel, but when they know they're going home, back to their familiar surroundings, they seem to go faster and instead of taking almost three days to cover the distance, we made it in two and half. It was getting dark by the time we came in sight of the village that we had sent a rider ahead to let them know we were coming in.

When we arrived, the village was all in festive mode. A large bonfire had been built in the center of gathering, and everyone was awake and eager to hear the stories of our hunt. When they saw the amount of meat that we brought in they were all amazed. We finally had so much meat that we had to build an extra carryall that we attached behind one of the riding horses, dragging the heavy meat along behind him.

I estimate that we probably had somewhere between five hundred and a thousand pounds of good moose meat for the tribe that winter. It was well appreciated by Chief Rolling Thunder and his family as well as by all the other hundred families in the village. As we ate that evening around the fire and I sat with my wife at my side, I was pleased at how Little Hawk managed to tell the story of the hunt.

Clyde was sitting on one side of me and Little Fire on the other and as he told the story of how the wolf pack had come in to interfere with our hunt, he also told how Clyde and I had saved the horses and the hunt. To my surprise, he pulled up the wolf pelts that we had harvested there at the corral and everyone was in fascination and admiration of what we had accomplished. I felt a grand smile come over my face, knowing that Clyde and I had paid back something of what this tribe was giving us by accepting us into their homes and into their lives for a whole winter. It was a grand celebration that night, and it went on well past the middle of the night.

Chapter 18: Life in Winter

I enjoyed watching my wife doing her tasks around our mud hut. Occasionally, as when we were husking corn, she let me help out. One of the things that I was most interested in and Clyde told me to study up on this real careful like, was the parching of corn. I'd occasionally seen white men and even Indians chewing away at something that looked like corn but I didn't know what it was all about until I saw my wife beginning the process of parching corn.

She had given me some for the trail on the moose hunt, and I liked it so much that I made the mistake of sharing it with my friend Clyde Patterson. That got both of us started on wanting to understand more about how this corn thing worked. I told him about the corn sweetened drink that we had from time to time in my mud hut. He told me that he had shared some of it with his friends the bachelor Braves as we call them who gathered in his hut for games of chance.

I was very tired today after the moose hunt but I was also very eager to learn about this parching of the corn. From what I could tell it started off with dried kernels of corn. I had counted roughly about a hundred ears of corn in our food storage that winter. We had already started to shuck some of the corn, removing the dried kernels and placing them in baskets for further drying.

Now my wife informed me that it was time to "cook the corn," as she called it. Obviously I'd had boiled corn often and considered it certainly one of the best foods that we had on the frontier. She had taken over my frying pan which I had purchased, I heavy metal thing I bought at Jacob Astor's trading post on the Arkansas River. She loved to use it for different things, including baking pan bread and even corn cakes and once I shared with her some bacon that we had brought with us from Feldman's trading post. She obviously really liked the bacon!

She prepared the frying pan with bear grease over the fire until we could smell the grease cooking and then she spread out over the frying pan a covering of corn kernels. She gently stirred the corn kernels with a wooden spoon moving them about gently so that the heat from the fire wouldn't burn them to the surface of the frying pan. Now I could begin to smell the sweet pungent odor of the corn as it was cooking.

Little Fire kept moving the corn about so that there was just one level of kernels on the pan and they were constantly being spread around as they cooked. I watched with fascination as the color of the corn, which for the most part had been a light yellow color, began to turn a reddish brown. She had spread a linen cloth on a flat board next to the fire and once the corn had turned that rich color that was reddish-brown, she took the kernels and scraped them on to the cloth to let the oil clear way.

I was too eager to taste the cooked corn and burned my finger trying to grab a piece of it off the pile. Little Fire scowled at me as though I were a naughty child and we both laughed as I popped the parched corn into my mouth and chewed with a big smile. Busy as ever, she went back to the same process making sure the pan was well oiled before she placed another covering of corn kernels over the entire surface of the frying pan. Once again, that delightful smell filled our hut and she continue to stir gently as the kernels turned that magnificent reddish brown color.

She did this all morning until finally she had a full basket of parched corn that we could use to supplement our food and take with us on our journeys. By the end of the day we had finished all hundred ears of corn that had been left drying there in the hut. I realized that the secret of the whole process was making sure that the corn was well dried and that might take several months of waiting. The result was magnificent nonetheless, and the parched corn served not only as a food but also as a flavoring for a wonderful drink. We would put the corn in a gourd of freshwater and let it sit for a while until its sweet taste permeated the entire container of water.

It was our favorite drink for celebrations there at home in our hut and one that we enjoyed sharing with others when it was time for a tribal celebration.

Chapter 19: Sam the Baker

There were several things I learned that winter in the Mandan Village, taught mostly by my wife, Little Fire. The parched corn was certainly a magnificent addition to my repertoire of frontier skills. There were very few mountain men that I knew who had the capability of cooking something as magnificent as parched corn. Most mountain men were content with their stews of bear meat and venison and didn't expect much more from life.

I was young and believed that there had to be more to food preparation than just that and I had already learned to make some pretty fantastic biscuits, I must say. But now I was interested in what the Mandan had been doing for generations, using various forms of flour, some even made from squash and of course, corn. Corn bread had been a favorite on the frontier in Illinois when I was growing up and putting honey on cornbread was probably just about the fanciest and finest thing I had ever tasted as a young boy!

The Indians use flour made from wild rice and some forms of meadow wheat as well as barley but their greatest source of flour was corn. Once they dried the corn, they would mash it into a find fine dust that then they could use as flour and they made with it pan breads and cakes there were actually quite tasty. At first I thought their pan bread tasted more like paper but with time I began to appreciate mixing venison gravy or bacon grease or bear grease and giving the pan bread a different taste.

Just as I had done with the parching of the corn, I watched Little Fire as she baked pan bread, literally every day. It was always easier to carry flour when traveling and mixing it with water and simply cooking it on a skillet was all that was required. I've seen her use flat rocks as a means of baking the pan bread and saw it rise as it turned a magnificent light brown color.

The use of berries and sunflower seeds was also a new discovery for me. I had already learned the value of pine seeds and was pleased to learn about pinon nuts. They were another close relative of the pine seed and provided an excellent source of protein as my mother called it. This made it possible to supplement our diet at times when animal flesh: deer and antelope, elk or bear was not available.

The pinion nuts were also a tasty addition to my diet. I preferred to crack the nut's shell and get at the kernel within, which to me tasted excellent. Some of the men had developed different way of enjoying the pinion nuts. They would chew them in the shell and one of them explained to me that they just swallowed the husks and all, it was easier than separating out the kernel! I never could get used to that!

As I watched my wife working with the heavy wooden ladle, stirring the parching corn across the skillet, I said to myself there must be a better tool for that. I knew just where to get the answer to my question. I went to my friend Clyde and asked him, "Could you make a flat long-handled tool for stirring the parched corn on the skillet? I don't mean a spoon, just a flat piece of wood would do the trick just fine, a few inches across and very thin!" I asked.

"Sure, let's go down to the wood pile and see if we can find us a nice long piece of maple, that would be the best wood to work with since its grain is smooth and long. We walked over to the wood pile at the far end of the palisade and found some longer pieces of wood that we could split and took them down to the length and thickness we desired. Clyde didn't carry his woodworking tools with him, they had stayed up at the cabin in the southern Rockies. But leave it to Clyde, he had made friends with the bowyer in the village.

Like so many things in the Mandan culture, the making of bows and arrows had become the personal domain of an Indian family. They had many tools that had been gathered from their ancestors and also, I might add, either purchased or stolen from white men along the frontier. I went with Clyde because I too was fascinated with the idea of developing skills like bow making and arrow making. Having been left abandoned in the wilderness on two occasions and having to make whatever tools I could to survive with from the trees of the forest, the idea of making a bow and arrow had always fascinated me.

The Indians took things from nature and perfected them into tools and weapons with amazing alacrity. As I looked around the hut of Raven's Wing, the bowmaker, I was impressed with all the various wood staves and arrow shafts that were everywhere. The whole hut seemed to be filled with bow and arrow making equipment and materials. There were bows in various stages of development that were magnificent. Some of them were long but most were shorter, making them easier to handle, especially on horseback.

In no time at all, Clyde was busy at work making the spatula that I had requested. And the smell of wood shavings soon filled the atmosphere in the hut. He had worked his magic as usual and the spatula was perfect. We applied some special oil that Raven's Wing had concocted from various sources, both from trees and from animals. We rubbed it into the wood and the white maple tone took on a rich golden color. My wife was going to be delighted!

Chapter 20: Daily Tasks

Certainly one of the most surprising things that I found in my Mandan hut when I moved in with my new wife, was the Buffalo boat. Not being familiar with the way things were on the Missouri River, I don't think I'd ever seen one before. To my surprise, every hut had its own boat made of buffalo skins and pine pitch and finely arched maple or oak branches. The boat was big enough for just two people and a little cargo, I guessed.

My wife invited me along for a trip across the river where she was going to fetch bundles of kindling from the nearby forest on the other side. There was a very nice stand of hardwoods on the opposite side of the Missouri from our camp and the women went back and forth across the river in their little boats. I've been watching them with fascination and wondered if I would ever be invited to join in the task of gathering firewood!

Today was my day, and just as the morning sun was coming down across the river we put our boat in the water and jumped in. It was a strange feeling because the boat seem to go in every direction at once and Little Fire was very adept at using her paddle to keep it on course moving directly across the river. Whenever the current took us we would slip quite a few feet downstream and she had to paddle in a certain direction to get us back on course.

I was clearly a novice at this action of paddling the boat, but I was there with an experienced boat woman. My experience with canoes made this buffalo boat seem strange indeed. With a canoe you always had a sense of its direction, even when you were off course! It was really fascinating to see how this little buffalo boat floated so well and hardly took in any water at all through its seams. It took us about fifteen minutes to cross the river, which at that level of its development was about two hundred yards across.

I could tell from the strain on Little Fire's face, that it'd taken quite a bit of effort to get me, her cargo, across the river. It felt good to be standing on solid ground as we disembarked on the opposite shore. We each had a small axe with us for gathering firewood and she had brought a few strands of deerskin rope to bind up the kindling we would be gathering.

The forest felt good, and soon we were scavenging for dry wood, of which there was an abundance because a storm had come through the year before and taken out quite a few of the young trees. They had been left there to dry, uprooted by the wind and the heavy rains. Some years the rain along the river made the ground in the riverbed and the river bottom very soft and soggy loosening the roots of the trees. If a good windstorm came across the prairie and the ground was very wet and soggy, trees were going to go down and that's what had happened the year before.

We worked through the morning and Little Fire had brought a small meal for us of pemmican and cornbread with a small gourd of sweetened corn water. We found a small clearing in the middle of the forest where we sat down with our backs against the trees and talked about our life. For just a few moments we felt isolated, and alone and I wondered what it would be like, just the two of us living on our own in the wilderness. We talked for a while about other members of the village and about Clyde and then things got very silent as though we had not ever entered that zone of talking before.

In fact, even though we had been living alone together in our hut for several months now, we were still novices at this business of being a couple. As I observed the other members of the village, I could tell that each couple had a different way of dealing with this kind of closeness. For some reason, I was sensitive to the way men and women dealt with one another as couples. Perhaps I had tried to figure out some meaning to my father's life after he married Miss Emily, but I never did.

That effort had made me more conscious of how men treated their wives and equally, how wives treated their husbands. Marriage was a very important thing in the Mandan culture, in fact it seemed as though their entire social reality was based around that important contract between man and wife. So here we were, Little Fire, my wife, and I with nothing to say! She was the first to enter that sacred territory, where I, Sam the Warrior, the Deer Slayer, was frightened to venture. "Are you happy Sam?" She asked, facing me and looking me directly in the eye.

No one had ever asked me such a personal and profound question before, especially with the sincerity that she put into it and I was befuddled for a moment, not knowing what to say. I thought about it for a while and I could feel the tension in her body as she sat there wondering what I was going to say to her. She was well aware of how fragile relationships between mountain men and native women could be, she had seen it before, and that frightened her, I believe.

"My life has been one long struggle, Little Fire. As I told you, my mother died when I was eleven years old and from that point on, I felt like someone wandering alone in the world. But here with you and among your people I have found a home. Honestly, I'm not sure if I would know when I was happy, I'm not sure I've ever been happy! But you have a right to know how I feel right now, so I will tell you, yes I am happy!" I replied and I could feel the tears coming to my eyes as I said it, because I knew I meant every word.

She seemed relieved by that I could tell from her face that she needed to know. I also could tell that we had crossed some grand barrier that lay between us. We would never have to cross it again.

Chapter 21: Clyde the Bow Maker

The wooden spatula that I gave to my wife brought a look of surprise and happiness to her face that I had not expected. She right away began playing with it in the air as though she were moving around parched corn on the frying pan, while dancing about in the middle of our hut. I sat back and just laughed and watched her perform her little spatula dance, it was delightful. I only wish that Clyde had been there to see it, though I did give him credit for having made that magical wand.

But that spatula introduced me to the bow maker's hut, which was one of the most amazing places I have ever been in in my life. As a child, my mother had told me fairy tales that had put images of such workshops in my mind. I have been to blacksmith shops and woodworking shops on the frontier before, both in Illinois and in Missouri and in the Colorado territories. But the bow maker's hut at the Slanting Village was something unique unto itself. My first introduction to the hut was when we went over to use his tools and work on the spatula. Clyde had made good friends with this man who was a genius with woodworking tools.

One day, when we both had some time on our hands, Clyde and I decided to go spend the day with the bow maker in his workshop hut. Clyde had found out that Raven's Wing was so obsessed with his bow making equipment that he had literally driven his wife out of their hut and now what had been originally their home, had become instead overwhelmed by the number of pieces of wood and arrows that were everywhere.

The bow maker had ingeniously created racks for himself for all of his equipment and his supplies. There were racks where you could see hundreds and hundreds of shafts of wood that would one day become arrows with lethal power to kill. There were racks where there were long staves of osage and ash and maple drying for future use as bows.

He was experimenting at this time with recurved bows, something that I had rarely ever seen on the frontier. When you are fighting Indians on horseback or from cover of the forest or the mountainside, you rarely paid attention as to whether they were using the straight bow or a recurve, you just wanted to stay out of the way of those damn arrows!

When we walked into the bow maker's hut that day he was there working a stave for a bow and Clyde and I immediately sat down on a low bench that he had next to his worktable. He was working with a light axe that he was using to trim down the face of the bow stave. It was amazing the skill that he had with that axe and I'm not sure whether he was using it to chip the stave down or shave it down, because he was doing a little bit of both. He kept swinging the axe in very short but very careful movements, taking small slivers and shavings from the stave in a very rapid but skillful manner.

When he had done one side, one half of the stave, he swung it over in his hand almost like a baton, and began doing the same thing on the other side working his way up. He started at first by taking some of the heavier chunks of wood from the stave and then he began seriously working the full length of the stave from the middle toward the tip.

Clyde and I both knew that the tips are where the most sensitive part of the entire operation was. One missed strike with the axe and the tip would break as it became more and more thin toward the far end at the bottom. Raven's Wing continued to work at that rapid skillful pace, smiling and talking to us as though he could do all of this at once without effort. "So, my friends, you are interested in making bows and arrows? You will use the great thunder sticks to kill and wound and hunt, but you want to learn to make bows and arrows, is in this craziness?" The bow maker asked smiling as he worked.

He was asking the question but he already knew the answer because we had told him before of our interest in his skill and his ability. We were completely engrossed in what he was doing, it was fascinating to watch a master at work.

Chapter 22: Learning the Skill

Raven's Wing was so pleased that we were willing to spend time in his shop, that he even offered to put us to work! My friend, Little Hawk, once told me that the bowyer and his family had been making weapons for the tribe since anyone could remember. Every young man had to come to Raven's Wing to be outfitted with a fighting bow when he reached the age of fourteen. The bowyer was also the training instructor for the village, making sure that the tradition of the war bow was kept alive by the people.

I was beginning to understand why these warriors were so proficient in the use of their weapons. I had seen the warriors of Running Wolf shoot accurately from a galloping horse. I had watched as one of my fellow mountain men was struck in the eye by an arrow that was shot through a rifle slot in a palisade wall! At the time, I considered it a lucky shot, unlucky for the poor young mountain man who lost his eye. But now I was starting to re consider that opinion. It might well have been an accurate shot after all, even from a galloping horse!

For many generations and perhaps for hundreds of years, the bow and arrow had been the privileged weapon of the Native American warrior. It was giving way now to the use of firearms, which the Indians called thunder sticks. But men like Raven's Wing were too proud to admit that the bow would ever be replaced by these mechanical things. There was something organic about the bow and arrow, it came directly from nature and working the wood required a respect for nature and an understanding of what it meant.

For the bow maker, the stave was something produced in the forest and at home in the forest. As a weapon of hunting it truly endowed a man with its special natural powers. At times he would wax eloquent on such matters as though he were defending his cherished child, archery, against the onslaught of progress and civilization. It was amazing how many ways the white man's world was invading and overwhelming what had been the natural way for Native Americans for hundreds of years!

As we sat in the workshop of the bow maker, we could feel the tension of history remaking itself, both fighting back and giving way against the flow of progress. This place of bow making and arrow making seem far removed from the world of muskets and rifles and pistols and shotguns and even cannons. Here, there was only the old ways, the way of the bow and the arrow, of the hatchet and the spear, the way of the knife and hand-to-hand combat. It was a time when men looked one another in the eye and fought to the death.

In the light of this type of warfare, fighting with cannons and rifles seemed very distant and sterile. There was something visceral about the knife and the hatchet and the tomahawk and the spear. I suppose that since the first use of the bow and arrow distant fighting and distant killing became a reality. My mother had told me many stories of the great English longbow and how it dominated history for hundreds of years in Europe. She loved to tell the stories of the battles of Agincourt and Crecy and how the rain of arrows had devastated the chivalry of France during the Hundred Years War.

Those were history lessons that I never forgot and the images that they conjured up in my mind would always be there. Whether she knew it or not, and I suspect she did, my mother was a great teacher, her lessons have stayed with me to this day more than ten years after her death. While these thoughts were drifting through my mind that morning in the bow maker's hut I realized he had put down the hatchet that he used to shape the rough staves of the bow.

I picked it up and looked carefully at the way it was tapered and realize that it was indeed a special ax head and the blade was fine, almost like a knife blade. I ran the tip of my finger along the blade to test its sharpness and immediately a small trickle of blood oozed out for my finger where the blade of the axe sliced through my skin without my putting any pressure on it at all. That brought a huge smile to the face of Raven's Wing and he nodded vigorously with pride at how sharp his axe was.

Chapter 23: Shaping the Stave

The bow maker gave us each of us a stave to work as he continued to work the one he had on his workbench. We stood at chopping blocks that were higher than usual, designed to serve for the shaping of the bow stave. I soon realized that my hatchet, in which I took such great pride, needed sharpening very badly. There was a whetstone there and I began to vigorously work the edge of my hatchet until it was sharp enough to do the same kind of work I was seeing done by the bow maker.

Now the chips are flying everywhere and the floor was covered as we continued to work all three bow staves at once. I was surprised at how easy it was and yet how careful you had to be not to take too much with one strike of the axe head. There was indeed a skill and an art to doing it properly and one had to always be thinking about the full length of what would become the bow arm.

As you made progress, gradually you were not chipping away anymore, you were shaving and that was an interesting part of the process, one that was very satisfying because it brought out the natural fiber of the wood. The bow maker explained to us how to recognize the natural tendency of the stave that we were working with so that we would be creating the proper bend orientation. He showed us how to position each end of the rough stave on the ground and apply pressure at its center pulling back on the top of the stave to flex it and identify the natural curve of that particular piece of wood. We were to work from there, creating the arms and the handle in the center.

What he was saying to us was that you let the piece of wood tell you what it wants to do and how it wants to be and how you should handle it. I said to Clyde that he was as good at reading a piece of wood as we white men were at reading books. We let the books teach us and tell us what we needed to know and Raven's Wing did the same with a piece of hickory or ash or cedar or Osage orange. We knew we were in the presence of a true master, someone who had done this same process hundreds and hundreds of times.

Every lesson we ever got from Raven's Wing however, began with the acknowledgment that he had misread his first bow stave and it broke the first time he tried to pull it back, using a rawhide cord. He explained to us that this had been his first lesson and that he had wept as a child over his failure. His father pointed out to him that he had misread the wood because he had not seen that there were significant boreholes and worm channels in the wood. He said they were so tiny he didn't believe they could be important but when the stave broke it broke right there where the bugs had eaten it away with their tiny channels.

I was very careful to inspect my bow stave then to make sure that the same thing wouldn't happen to me and the piece of wood that I had, one of the yellow woods, I believe it was a locust wood, had no signs of insects boring into its heart. The bow maker had explained to us that if the lines ran parallel to the fiber of the wood that these could be eliminated very easily and would not affect the strength of the wood when it was bent back and compressed. It was the boreholes that went straight through that were the problem, he explained.

After about an hour the three of us had shaped our respective bow staves and roughed out what were the equivalent of three longbows easily five feet in length. I found it very gratifying to see, looking at the handle and the two arms of my stave, that I already had a rough image of a bow right there in my hand!

Now, according to the bow maker it was just a matter of finishing the work and that was done by shaving, almost like whittling with the knife give it a final shape. We used our heavy hunting knives for this part of the work. Scraping down and shaving down the two arms of the bow, was done by drawing the knife as though it were a two handled scraping tool. I held the handle with my left hand and with my right I wrapped a bandanna around the tip and used the knife as a drawing, cutting tool to take off the thin fibers of shavings.

The bowyer had a fascinating method for the final shaping of the bow. He had taken deer hide and put a surface of glue on it and then sprinkled sand from the stream bed near the Missouri so that a rough surface was created. When you rubbed the surface of the bow, it made the rough places where the knife had been, smooth and perfect. Even Clyde was impressed with this creation of the bow maker!

Chapter 24: Drawing the Bow

The final process of making the tips of the bow ready for the string was the most delicate part of bow making. Each end of the bow had to be perfectly the same and made with a gentle cut into the sides at the end so that the string would fit perfectly into the nock and stretch out along the length of the bow when it was pulled tight. It was natural to make the handle of the bow the same size as my own hand and I realized how personal this bow was becoming for me, I was making it to my own dimensions!

Once the wood had been fully shaped and worked down to its bending quality, I was surprised at how light the bow actually was and how easy to carry. I had become so used to carrying the ten pound musket, my favorite Hawken rifle, that it never occurred to me that I might be carrying a weapon as lethal that weighed hardly a fifth of what the rifle weighed. There was a lot to learn from the way the Native Americans waged battle and used weapons.

We went on from there to learn to make arrows and one whole section of the hut of the bow maker was dedicated to sheaves of sticks that would one day become arrows. Every warrior carried at least a dozen arrows in his quiver going into battle and most of them preferred to have more than that. Each arrow had to be made by hand and some of them had to be adjusted because of their shape.

Arrows could be selected from woods as diverse as witch hazel and fennel and dogwood and even ash or hickory. What is important in selecting woods for arrows is that they be without knots or shoots. We were given instruction that morning about how to straighten an arrow shaft, which was something that I'd never considered. But nearly every one of the shafts that we found required some adjustment, as they were crooked.

There was always a fire burning in the bow maker's hut and it was that fire that served us as a way of straightening the arrows. The spot where the bend was in the shaft would be heated gently over the fire. Once it was warm, you could bend it across your knee to adjust it to a perfect straight line. It was held that way as it cooled and a straight arrow was produced!

I was fascinated with the way the nock was developed in the end of the arrow where the string would be placed against the arrow. Raven's Wing preferred to re-enforce that opening with fine sinew and knot it down tight in order to prevent any chance of the arrow shattering when the string was released. Every single aspect of the bow's performance had to be considered right down to the effect that the force of the bow would have on the backend of the arrow.

A large basket held all the arrow heads that the master bow maker had on hand. There were steel arrow heads and stone arrowheads there, and we were told to make a choice of which ones we preferred. Clyde chose a steel one that obviously had been made in some blacksmith shop somewhere. For my part, I chose the stone ones, favoring the more natural way of the ancient warriors. Using our knives, we cut the front end of the arrow making a slot where the arrowhead shank would go in and once again wrapped it with sinew which was then heated and glued tight around the shank of the arrowhead.

It was late afternoon by the time we finally left the bow maker's hut and as Clyde and I looked at one another we realized that we had been given an entire lesson not only in making of the bows but also making arrows. We were told to come back the next day and finish our project as our bow was just about ready for its oiling process. Raven's Wing always carefully finished his bows with a special oil process that he had derived from bear grease and pine pitch and many other sources.

Whenever you were in his hut you could smell the warming oil in his little pot near the fire. He would heat it up intensely when he needed to but otherwise it was kept there, always warm in his little pot. He was very proud of his concoction, whatever was in it, no one really knew.

Chapter 25: Finished Bows

Clyde and I were right back at the bow maker's hut after breakfast the next morning. We were both excited about our accomplishment of the day before, realizing that we had literally made a primitive weapon out of raw materials. Now would be time to string the bow and begin its flexing process. The Indians had been making very strong hemp strings and ropes from natural fiber for a long time.

Raven's Wing believed in using well-seasoned hemp and he had a special wax that he put on it that he rubbed over and over again to keep the string dry against rain and humidity. The elements of weather were never completely favorable to the warrior's quest in hunting or in battle. You always had to be ready for anything. He helped us tie off the strings making a special loop for one end and then tying down the other with a slipknot.

Now the bows were ready for action and we spent the morning making more arrows. Once you got the process down, making arrows was easy, it just took time, since each arrow had to be treated separately. By noon the second day we had half a dozen arrows each and we were ready to test out our new well-oiled weapons.

Out behind the hut of the bow maker there was an archery range set up for young men to practice and on any given day you would usually find several of the young warriors in training there. They first pulled the bow when they were about five or six years old, so they had been doing this very early on. The bow maker explained to us that what was most difficult in the training process was when a boy began to develop bad habits in his use of the "bows of childhood" as he called them.

Raven's Wing explained to us that there were two kinds of human beings, one kind that was more calculating and reserved while the other was more impulsive and aggressive. Each type had to be handled differently in training he said. It was very important not to try to change the nature of an individual. I was impressed with his wisdom and understood that he was absolutely correct in his understanding of human nature.

He was as eager as we were to see the results of our work and he was also testing out the bow that he had just made. As we stood at the shooting line and looked down the range at the targets made of straw we could see white painted targets made of deerskin wrapped around the straw packed heavy and tight. My first shot went wild, well over the target, but I was pleased that my bow had performed well under pressure. It had not broken!

I knew for my second shot that I had to bring the arrow down and keep it from sailing high over the target and hitting up against the palisade behind the end of the shooting range. My second arrow came much closer to the target though it still went over by six inches. It was the third arrow that finally struck the target and I noticed out of the corner of my eye the Clyde was having the same problem I was having, overshooting by several inches. Finally, we both compensated and settled down and under the trained eye of the bow maker, we were soon shooting well within the range of the target. Fingers began to hurt as they were not used to this kind of activity. Raven's Wing told us that that was normal, everyone had a hard time at first.

"With time you will develop calluses on your fingers and you will be surprised at the strength your hand and develops in the pulling of the bow. The same is true of your shoulders and chest muscles you will become a stronger man for exercising in this manner!" He said chuckling to himself as he walked away from the shooting range. Clyde and I looked at each other with satisfaction and felt that we had come a long way in understanding the culture of the Mandan tribe.

I'd watched Little Hawk practicing at the shooting range and was very impressed with his skill, but even more so with speed at which he could lose arrows. Sometimes you actually had to look twice to make sure that you had seen what you had seen. His hand movements were so fast even when he was walking or running or riding his pony, that if you didn't pay attention, you might miss the fact that he had shot three arrows when you thought he only shot one!

Chapter 26: Early Spring

The days were getting warmer now and the winds off the great River became soft and less biting. During the winter months, the fierce winds across the prairie and the river sometimes felt like they were cutting into your skin. A good wind could reduce the cold temperature down probably ten degrees making it more difficult to move about outside. I found a shallow passage across the Missouri where it bent toward the south and now I had access to the forests on the other side which were promising because I knew that they held several large herds of deer.

By this time, so late in the winter, it was good to have extra fresh meat for the village so I decided to go out every day and see if I could take some deer in the woodlands that extended out on the eastern bank of the great River. Some days, Clyde came with me and some days it was Little Hawk who would join me on my hunt. The days that I enjoyed the most were the quiet solitary ones where I was out hunting alone.

I came to know the habits of the deer from observing them on a regular basis over several weeks' time. They were creatures of habit just as we humans were creatures of habit. They followed the same trails and foraged in the same feeding areas. Once I got to know their habits of feeding I could plan my hunts on a regular basis. There were two large deer herds in that forested area, each herd having upwards of seventy-five deer.

I spent several days observing both herds and getting to know the make up, the ages of the various animals which I'd come to understand now from my experience hunting deer. I could pretty much tell you exactly the age of a young buck or whether a doe was about to drop a fawn. I considered the herd a wealth for the village, something to cultivate and not to abuse or destroy. Because of that, I chose specific deer from the herd, a mature buck or an older doe.

Once I figured out the patterns of both herds I would go out early before sunrise and get set up at their usual feeding places and take down two deer and field dress them there on the spot, making a travois to carry the meat back to the village. Challenger gradually became comfortable with this unusual extra weight. She even got used to dragging the travois back over the Missouri.

The women of the village were pleased with the results of my hunts and I made sure that Little Fire got the choice rump steaks for our evening meals. After about two weeks of this regular hunting, I was called into the Chief's hut, as usual not sure exactly why I was being summoned.

Chief Rolling Thunder began with the smoking of the pipe and after he had taken several good draws on the pipe he handed it to me and begin speaking, "My son the Deer Slayer! You have once again shown me the value of your presence here in our village. Providing food for the community here is well appreciated. As you know many in our village are sick at this time of year, with the long winter and the dwindling food supplies. We have lost many members over the past few years and our numbers have gone down considerably!" He said taking the pipe back and taking another draw on it looking into the fire in his usual thoughtful way.

I was well aware of the sickness in the village and already since the Buffalo camp I'd seen over a dozen members die, often of the white man's illness, as the Indians called it. We had already buried five people that month and the burial mounds on the hill beside the village were growing in numbers. The Mandan had their own way of burying the dead, the body was placed on a high platform and the family grieved for four days there. Once the body decayed and the skeleton was left, the bones were interred, except for the skull which was placed on a circle mound near the village.

It was one of the most startling things about life in the Mandan Village, that there was this strange mound off to the northeast of the village. Family members would go out to the spot where the skull of their loved one was and often would speak to that family member as though they were still alive and still there. I found it very touching, this way of grieving that was so much a part of their tradition. As I thought of my mother's death, I guess that's what Pa and I were doing every Sunday after church when we went to her grave and "paid our respects," as Pa used to say.

Chapter 27: Leave the Village

The spring of eighteen twenty-six was particularly harsh for the Mandan of the Slanted Village. So many people died of the smallpox that year that Clyde and I began to worry about staying amid so much illness. In my conversation with Chief Rolling Thunder, he asked me about my plans for the coming season. His question was very specific because he said to me, "Would you take my daughter with you, away from all this illness, away from her people who are suffering and dying in such great numbers?"

I hadn't thought of having to deal with such a dire prospect, but every day that spring things seems to get worse and Little Fire and I spoke of it often, as though there were no solution. One night I finally spoke with her about what her father had said, "My wife, we do have a choice to make here. You and I could leave the village and go back to the trap lines that I have been following for the past two years. Clyde and myself are well-versed in that life of the trapper and I would be willing to take you with us on the trap line, if you agree," I said this hesitantly knowing that the life of a young Indian woman is closely tied to the allegiance of her family and her village.

Her brother Little Hawk and I had spoken about the fact that if the numbers continue to go down in the village, that Chief Rolling Thunder would have no choice but to

88

move his people and join with the Hidatsa, a similar tribe, living closer to the mountains. These villages were spared from the "face-eating disease" as it was called, because they were not exposed to the riverboats coming up the Missouri. All of this seemed to be happening very fast and I wasn't expecting to have to make a decision like this, I had given it very little thought. As the illness progressed from one hut to the next, I realize how dangerous it was to be living so close together, exposed to those who were suffering such mortal illness.

We didn't understand fully how dangerous it was and how important it would've been to quarantine those who were sick so that they did not transmit the disease to others. Clyde and I had a conversation about it and he was already determined to leave, he had spoken with Chief Rolling Thunder about it already. It was terrible to see the children dying of this plague and soon the families gave up the traditional way of caring for the dead and simply placed them in a large vacant mud hut, body beside body on the ground and left them there, wrapped in buffalo robes.

I helped to carry one of the children into that terrible place and the stench was unbearable, even though the bodies were wrapped in heavy buffalo robes. It was a frightening place for anyone to visit and I only went there because I had promised to carry the body of the little girl into that place of burial for those who died of the illness. It was a frightening time and I couldn't bear to be there for any length of time, I was out that place in a hurry! Little Fire was waiting for me outside and weeping for the child who had lost her life fighting the white man's sickness.

It was that night that we began to plan our journey away from the village, away from centuries of tradition and all the family togetherness that made life so beautiful for those living in the village. It was hard to admit that the village itself was dying and that what it stood for no longer meant anything, except a place of suffering and death. The chief and his counsel had already determined that they would leave that place of sickness behind and go to live with their kindred tribe, the Hidatsa. It was now just a matter of timing. Clyde and I got our belongings together and took some of the food that we had left from the winter reserves. We loaded up both our pack horses and Horace, and prepared to leave.

I was gratified that Little Fire chose to leave with me and we promised her parents and her brother that we would be back to visit during the Buffalo hunt that summer. It was a sad day when we left, though the spring was now in its full warmth. The ice along the edges of the river was melting and it had been two weeks since the last snowfall. Clyde and I decided to stop at nearby Fort Union where we could purchase traps at the trading post there, and head back into the mountains to set our trap lines.

Taking my wife with me was one thing that I could cling to as satisfying. We had set up a life of our own, we were an entity together, and I felt that we belonged with one another. My winter within the Mandan Village helped me to understand what she was leaving behind. There was a closeness and intimacy about life in an Indian village that no white man could ever understand. I was able to observe some of it and I was trying to understand what she was giving up to go with me. I was glad that I could speak her language, that made a difference.

Chapter 28: Trapping Again

Chief Rolling Thunder and the main body of the Mandan were moving out at the same time as we did and heading west toward the villages of the Hidatsa away from the western Missouri. Clyde and I had decided we would head for Fort Union which was now a thriving trading post set up by Mackenzie and Astor near the Montana territory. We still had a few of our traps from our previous expeditions but not enough to do any serious beaver work.

Beaver was still paying seven dollars a pelt, which for us meant that we could continue to make a good living trapping beaver. We estimated that it would take us well over a week to reach the Mackenzie trading post at Fort Union, but we knew that there we could obtain the supplies and traps that we needed. We had plenty of money left over from our previous year's trapping and our winnings at the rendezvous.

The village people were traveling slowly and so we went ahead, telling Little Hawk that we would always be there if they needed us, to just send a rider. There was no danger of hostility toward a tribe that have been infected with the white man's disease. Even their enemies, the Lakota, would not trouble them now, for fear of the illness. It was a terrible and humiliating thing for a tribe to be considered outcasts in their own land!

It was the plan of Chief Rolling Thunder that they would reconstitute their people and their dignity near the village of the Hidatsa, eventually becoming part of that tribe. They hoped that getting away from the place of contagion where they had been living at the Slanted Village, that they might escape the contagion of the illness. It was a terrible journey, even though the weather was bright and even cheery. Spring was in full blossom and the rivers were high because of the snow melt.

Clyde and Little Fire and I continued on our way toward the trading post and made it there by the end of that first week. Everything was bustling at the trading post and we were careful not to mention that we had come from the Slanted Village which everyone in the frontier knew had been devastated by the smallpox. The Indians called it the "wasting face disease" because of the way the pox affected the faces of those it killed.

We were glad to get back and purchase those things that made sense to the life of a trapper: bacon, beans and flour, tobacco and most especially coffee! We resupplied our ammunition and our gunpowder and purchased several bags of barley and oats for the horses and I even found a few turnips for the old mule. Horace was as cantankerous as ever and because I was out of turnips, it had not been a happy trip. Things would change now that I'd been able to purchase a few expensive turnips for that damn mule!

Our time at the trading post was also helpful in getting us information about how things were going in the Rocky Mountains that season. We found out that beaver was still selling well at the trading posts and if we were lucky we would probably be able to find a few streams still rich in beaver. Clyde ran into an old friend of his who told him about a Mountain Valley near the Yellowstone where there was plenty of beaver.

It would be a good distance for us to travel, probably at least two weeks' time, but for now, we had no other agenda, and so we decided to head for the Yellowstone. We would follow the Yellowstone into the heart of Wyoming territory and there we hoped to find this marvelous Valley Clyde's friend was telling about. We were familiar enough with the Gallatin area further south, and I was eager to see the Hot Springs that Yellowstone was now becoming known for.

Clyde reminded me that they were called Coulter's Hell in honor of his friend John Coulter who was probably the first white man to set foot in that valley. I sure wanted to see them, and as it turned out even my partner hadn't seen them!

Little Fire surprised me with her enthusiasm over such a journey, knowing that she had not traveled that far West in her young years. She was a hard worker, and Clyde appreciated everything she did around the camp. She kept things going when we were exhausted with travel. She seemed to have an unlimited amount of energy, something that we needed very badly as we traveled through the rough wilderness area. She proved to be a welcome addition to our team!

Chapter 29: Follow the Yellowstone

From Fort Union we followed the trail that skirted the Yellowstone toward the South. It was the direction that we needed to go in to find the high mountain valley described by Clyde's friend as a great source of beaver pelts. We passed through a small settlement that was being called Billings on our way and once again gathered information about Indian activity in the area as we were concerned especially about the Crow Indians.

The Blackfeet had been our nemesis so far in the Rocky Mountains territories to the east, and now that we were moving further west into the heart of the great mountains themselves, we had to be concerned about the raiding parties of Crow Indians moving about in the territory. Like the Blackfeet, the Crow were an especially aggressive tribe. They were jealous of their territory, their hunting grounds, as they called them. These boundaries were very hard to decipher, but it didn't keep the tribes from fighting one another over transgressions.

Clyde had several run-ins with the Crow Indians before I ever met up with him. He described one particular battle along the Missouri where the American army had come to settle a dispute over land north of Santa Fe. He told me that the Crow had fought to the death and that they had taken many casualties in the skirmish with the American army. He told me that we would have to stay clear of the Crow at any cost. Naturally, I asked my wife for her Native American understanding of that particular nation, and she just shook her head and wouldn't talk about it, she seemed genuinely frightened.

We were eager to get back to the high mountains where we felt that we could practice our beaver trade without the hindrance of war parties or the bickering over boundaries. At first it looked as though we were going to succeed in this, as we did find the Valley that Clyde's friend had spoken of. It was truly an amazing network of streams, beaver dams, and beaver lodges.

A fast flowing river cut the Valley between two mountain chains in the Bighorn region. Running off the mountainsides to the north and to the south there were large streams and waterfalls that came gushing down the valley. We were there in the best part of beaver hunting season, the early spring. The snow melt had caused the streams to be in full force as they fought their way down the valley, hurtling over rocks and cliffs, rushing toward the river below.

I will always recall that first moment as we crested the ridge that crossed into the valley itself, it was a bright spring day and you could literally hear the rushing water from across the valley floor. As we look down on the green and lush valley, we could see large pasture ranges where there were several herds of elk taking advantage of the sweetgrass already that early spring. There were still patches of snow here and there reminding us that we were not too far from what must've been a very severe winter at this high-altitude.

    I would estimate the mountain peaks on either side of this Valley at roughly 10,000 feet in height. There was still a lot of snow around the summits well above tree line. But for the most part, the valley walls were emptied of their snow cover. It had turned to water, and was now hurtling downward toward the river below in streams gushing with the cold water of early spring. For a trapper, looking into a valley like this was like finding a gold mine! Clyde and I were so excited we just began to smile at one another and we clasped hands from saddle to saddle and shouted our enthusiasm, our fists raised in the air.

    My wife couldn't quite understand why two men would become so boisterous and excited over just seeing another Rocky Mountains Valley. She knew that we had seen hundreds of such valleys in our time in the mountains and yet this one held a secret that she couldn't understand. Little Fire would learn soon enough what it meant for a trapper to find streams of this volume and this intensity.

    Clyde and I both knew that we had just found the beaver gold mine and we couldn't wait to get started. We understood all the work that was ahead of us for probably the next two months, possibly three, but we could make a fortune here. The Valley was far enough into the heart of the Bighorns that we knew we were protected from warring Indian tribes and war parties traveling about in the mountains. The Blackfeet and the Crow had their own hunting grounds for the elk migration. The small numbers of elk that we were seeing in this Valley indicated that this would probably be the final destination of such a migration. The Indians would stalk the herd at an earlier point of rendezvous, avoiding a lengthy journey this high into the mountains.

Chapter 30: Setting Camp

We spent almost an entire day scanning the Valley and glassing it with our field glass, hoping to be able to plan a complete trapping out of the valley. From where we sat on the crest of the Valley we could literally see the patterns of water rushing down from the snow melt above. Because the streams were all at their peak intensity from the snow melt, it was easy to see the network and where our best chances for beaver activity would be.

Every spring, this same pattern had been establishing itself probably for hundreds of years and we could see that families of beaver would seek out the best of these streams to set up their protective ponds damning the water up to protect their lodges from predators. Having observed this behavior over and over again for nearly three years now, I had come to know how the mind of the beaver worked. A trapper had to understand why beaver built dams, why they establish their lodges in certain places, and what the point of the whole thing was.

All the activity of the beaver was designed around two things: first of all the safety and security of their family hidden in its underground underwater Lodge. But secondly to procure a supply of good food, shoots from willows and aspens and Birch, tender softwoods that they could store for winter food supplies. Once a trapper understood this, then calculating the work of trapping and setting up trap lines, was a matter of consequence.

We first carefully counted the number of streams on either side of the Valley. We knew that eventually, by the time this season was over, we would have probably trapped out every single one of them. By our present count we figured that there must be at least five major streams on either side of the Valley and it would be very probable that these large streams all had beaver families working them. A valley like this allowed generations and generations of beaver to continue to expand their activity throughout the entire open space that now lay before us.

We camped at the upper edge of the Valley that night and had already designed our plan, moving first to the right, expecting to camp between the first two major streams on the north side of the Valley. As we held each other that night under the Buffalo robes, Little Fire and I shared the excitement of the moment and I tried to explain to her why this Valley was so unique and so amazing. Her people called beaver the "flat tails," and only harvested the pelts of the beaver for the purpose of building or creating warm robes and sometimes hats for winter wear.

It would never occur to them that harvesting beaver by the hundreds could be a lucrative business and a commercial venture that could make rich men of Clyde and myself. With time, she would understand how such commerce worked because she would have enough experiences in the trading posts like the one on the Santa Fe Trail or the one at Fort Union that we had just come through.

As she watched us trading and buying things at the trading posts I could tell she was learning, that she was beginning to understand how commerce worked among the white people.

Bartering among American Indians was a whole different thing and her people, the Mandan, had long been the great traders of the Missouri River. For many generations and perhaps for hundreds of years, the Mandan had been the tribe at the center of all trading among American Indians. The crops that they raised, corn and beans and sunflowers, the Buffalo robes that they gathered in such great numbers, became trading items that could be found all along the Missouri River.

I knew that my young wife would soon grasp the concept of the white man's commercial adventures along the frontier. For now, she seemed to just enjoy my excitement and soon we had exhausted ourselves in lovemaking and both of us fell sound asleep listening to the far distant sounds of the rushing water from the streams below. This Valley would be our life for the next three months at least.

Chapter 31: Setting Traps

From our ridge camp high above the valley, Clyde and I had identified a spot that looked like a large swamp on the northern side of the Valley and we headed there that morning as soon as sunrise and breakfast was over. It took us nearly half a day to reach that spot but when we got there it was exactly what we expected. We had hoped that the opening in the tree pattern was a sign of a beaver swamp created off of a major beaver dam.

That was exactly what we found when we got to that spot where the trees had fallen or been cut down by an aggressive beaver colony. When you first came upon such a devastation of midsized and large trees by a beaver colony, it was always a bit of a shock. The fact that these forty-pound animals could take down a twenty or thirty foot-high tree by simply chewing their way through almost a foot of solid wood, was a constant source of amazement.

When we pulled up to the large treeless opening on the mountainside, it was indeed as though some great storm had come through and just wiped out the trees for hundreds of yards. In fact, what we saw were stumps of trees and the trees had just simply disappeared! It didn't take long for us to find out where those trees had gone as we looked up and we could see that we were standing at the base of a beaver dam that rose almost ten feet from the ground on which we were standing.

As usually happens, the trees and branches and mud had grown over and grass had grown up along the outer side of the dam so that it looked as though you were standing next to a hillside or hillock. In fact behind that hill were thousands and thousands of gallons of water restrained by a meticulously built dam, constructed for purposes of beaver survival. Even my wife seemed surprised by the size of this damn and its extent across the small mouth of the canyon. It was indeed like a canyon where the water had carved a path through the hillside heading down from high above.

But the watercourse bottomed out into a large flat area where the trees had been cut down by the beavers and an amazing dam had been built, over eight feet in height, holding back an enormous amount of water and there right in the middle of this large body of water, animal-made, stood the beaver lodge. In my years as a trapper in the Rocky Mountains I've seen a lot of beaver lodges and some of them surprised me by their girth and their height. This one was bigger than any I'd ever seen and indicated that we were in the presence of an enormous beaver colony. Our efforts in coming this far into the mountains of this big wilderness were about to pay off.

We knew that off to the west, was another stream equally as big as this one and, we hoped, as busy with beaver activity as this one certainly was. It was important for us to explore this terrain before we decided to set up our camp though we already tentatively knew that our campsite would be halfway between one stream and the other. Our campsite would be the place where we would skin and butcher the beaver from either one of the colonies. We expected to set about fifteen traps in either one of the streams and hoped to gather at least twenty-five beaver from this one colony set up alone.

By early afternoon we had already found our campsite spot at a location where a small spring opened out of the side of the mountain and a little waterfall presented itself, with clear running water for the horses and for our needs. We explained to Little Fire that this is where we would build our camp and Clyde and I began unpacking the horses and the mule and they seemed happy to get settled into this new spot. There was plenty of grass growing there on the mountainside and a meadow just below us that we could use to feed the horses. It was a perfect spot for our camp and the view the valley below was phenomenal. Everything seems so green and so alive this early in the spring!

Before the afternoon was over Clyde and I had set ten traps at the first stream we had come to. I had no doubt that by the next day we would easily have taken at least three beaver in our traps. We were both exhausted by the time we bedded down that night and I was so tired I fell asleep before even felt my wife slide in next to me under the Buffalo robes. We were up at first light the next day ready to set traps in the second stream.

By noon, another set of ten traps had been set and we were ready to check the trap line at the first stream. The first three traps showed no results but by the fourth trap we found one of the largest beavers we had ever taken. She must have weighed at least fifty pounds, and her pelt was magnificent. We found two other beaver taken in the remaining traps. Three beaver on our first day, that was a good sign!

Chapter 32: Beaver Harvest

It surprised me how easy it was for Little Fire to integrate herself into the work of beaver trapping. Setting the traps and checking them every day was in some ways the easiest part of the work we had to do. The really difficult and demanding part of the work was the skinning and butchering of the animals as we took them from the traps. Their pelts had to be carefully removed first, and then stretched and carefully tended and treated on drying racks to preserve their natural luster and smooth flexibility.

From earliest childhood, Little Fire had watched this process go on, done almost exclusively by the women in her tribe. She took to this part of our trapping venture with ease and a natural skill that I must say put me to shame. I was more than happy to dig the flesh pits as we harvested these marvelous pelts and set them up to dry on the round racks. She was able to quickly put together a drying rack, which was nothing more than just a pole made from either Maple or Willow and then stitch the animal hides to the rack with leather thongs.

After the first day, where we harvested the three beaver, the numbers kept going up every day. We spend a full two weeks at our first encampment between the two large streams and by the time we were done, we had a dozen pelts drying and being treated for suppleness and flexibility. We then moved on to the other streams along that northern side of the Valley and as expected, spent another two weeks there, harvesting beaver from three streams at once. In less than a month's time we already had twenty-five beaver pelts and we have been careful to not diminish the colonies in such a way that they couldn't come back in one or two seasons.

We were now ready to move to the southern face of the Valley and we crossed the small river, which was probably about fifteen feet across and ran down from the eastern part of the Valley. We decided to take a day at the Riverside and just relax and bathe since we been working almost constantly for three or four weeks at our beaver trade. The results of our work were certainly among the best we'd ever taken. We knew that the streams on the southern side of the Valley would be equally as productive and require that much more work.

By now we were getting into the later part of the spring and the streams had slowed down some and we expected that the beaver activity might also slow down as well. We were wrong in that, as it turned out the beaver colonies on the southern mountainside were now actively trying to repair damage had been done to the dams during the snow melt rush of water coming down from the peaks above.

Where we had taken twenty-five beaver in the first month on the northern side of the Valley, we took thirty-five during that second month of June on the southern side of the Valley! We gave the pelts an extra week at the end of June to cure in the sunlight and we used various methods to keep the pelts fresh and lubricated. We used bear grease and also some brain substance that was considered to be the best of all the tanning oils.

By the end of June we had packed up our two animals with a heavy load of beaver pelts and we were ready now to head down to Fort Collins where a new trading post had been set up in memory of John and Jean Collins my friends who had been massacred there by the Comanches. We expected it would take us almost ten days to make it that far south but now we were in no hurry since we knew we had accomplished enough work in just two months to carry us for the whole year if need be.

It seemed as though our life as trappers was going to be like that every year. Several months of very intense daily labor, with little or no let up, followed by several months of inactivity when there was very little to be done as the beaver season wound down. We never knew how long it would last, the beaver trade, but for now it was a good way for us to make a living and we would continue for as long as it held up.

Chapter 33: Fort Collins

The country we traveled through on our way south toward Fort Collins was certainly among the most beautiful of the entire territory of the Rocky Mountains. Wherever you looked you could see snow-covered peaks and rushing rivers. We found several lakes on our way down from the Bighorns and I managed to see the Hot Springs in Yellowstone earlier that year. Little Fire and I were fascinated with the geysers of exploding hot water that seem to just rise out of the earth for no reason at all, and explode into the air in spray and mist and little rainbows.

That was certainly a memory that we would never forget. Another thing that really struck me in the Hot Springs area was the Buffalo wallows where the great beasts would settle into the hot mud and seemed to rise out of the mist like some ancient beast from a fairytale. Their snorting as they blew the mud from their nostrils is the kind of thing you'd never forget as long as you live!

It was mid-June when we reached Fort Collins and inquired about the rendezvous for that summer. We were told it was going to be at Popo Agie, near the Green River in the Wyoming territory. Clyde and I agreed that there was no possibility that we could miss another Green River rendezvous! But then we only had two weeks to get there and we explained to Little Fire what that meant and how we would be journeying back across the Mountain region called the Medicine Bow Mountains. She had always trusted the men of the tribe to plan travel and destinations, so she assured me that she would follow wherever the trail led.

Our trading at Fort Collins had gone well and the beaver pelts that we had to sell were considered top-quality and to our pleasant surprise, paid ten dollars a pelt. On previous trapping ventures, Clyde and I had split three hundred dollars and thought it was a lot of money, but this time we were splitting well over six hundred! I have to say that the amount of work that my wife did, should've earned her at least a third of that, but Clyde and I had not made an agreement of this type and Little Fire was in no position to argue with us about it. That would come later.

To settle up with her I gave her fifty dollars to spend at the trading post. She was so surprised by this windfall of money and very much unaware of what it meant that I had to coach her through every purchase at the beginning. After she had spent about ten dollars buying soap and combs and candy and beads, I knew she was ready to be on her own. I was impressed by the fact that she set aside twenty dollars of the remaining forty in a secret place in what she called her wampum pouch. She was catching on very quickly about how this thing worked, the white man's commerce!

We spent an enjoyable week at Fort Collins where a small community was already building up. Jean and John Collins would have been pleased. Some of the wagon trains had come up from Santa Fe Trail to settle in the region. People from the east seemed to appreciate the mild summer climate and once they got into the winter, it was too late to turn back and they simply had to adjust to ten feet of snow falling all around them. But with every little community like this all sorts of white man things began to build up, there were barbershops and general stores and what had been a trading post before now was becoming a small thriving community. Little Fire couldn't get enough of it all, she was so excited!

She quickly spent the other twenty dollars and was reluctant to fall back on her twenty dollar reserve, so I knew it was time for us to move on. Eventually, she would make a connection between the work that we did harvesting beaver and the money we had to spend at the trading posts and in the general stores, and then watch out!

The commander of the military outpost was an Irishman named McDoogle, I never did get his first name! He called me in one day because he had heard of my relationship with the Collins' who had first settled at that location. He didn't really know the details of the little trading post John Collins had set up there, so I told him what I knew about the couple. As a military man, he was especially curious about the Indian attack and how I had survived.

I told him the story as best I could, filling in the blanks about Horace my mule. He loved that part of the story and actually took notes about the Comanche war party. He wanted to know their numbers and the direction they were headed in, even though it was years ago now. I showed him the scars where they hit me with the tomahawk and how I escaped thanks to Horace. Now he was sure he had to see that damned mule, so we headed out to the corral.

Horace came trotting over to the fence where we stood, looking for his turnip ration and it just so happened I had a piece for him. Captain McDoogle watched in fascination as Horace chomped on the turnip, said he'd never seen a mule do that before! As usual, Horace let out a loud braying sound to tell me he wanted more, and when I shook my head negative, he blew out one of his loudest farts, which gave the Captain a fit of laughter. We parted as good friends nonetheless.

Chapter 34: Rendezvous Again!

It was July first when we set out from the Collins Trading Post and headed west across the Medicine Bow Range toward Green River and Popo Agie. We had some rough weather high in the mountains and it looked as though it was going to snow one of the days we were there! We were probably up at 10,000 feet, maybe even more, and as we looked out over the tree line below us, we could see the sputtering of snowflakes coming down from the higher altitudes.

Looking out in either direction North and South we could see snow-covered peaks where the snow never left and would stay there all summer long. The sun glistened on the icy covered peaks and it was kind of chilling because the winds at that altitude and the thin air made you wonder why you ever came up that high. It certainly made you think of getting down into a more normal temperature and climate right away!

Fortunately, we only had to spend one day up that high and then everything was downhill from there heading down into Wyoming territory following the Green River down to the place of the rendezvous. Our plans had foreseen about a week of travel and that's pretty much what it took us so that we were there just as the rendezvous was beginning to gather momentum. As before, the trading companies were already well-established the previous week and now the Bent brothers had joined Astor, Ashley and St. Vrain and were hawking their goods to the wild and chaotic world of the mountain man.

To me, the rendezvous was a very special expression in the life we lead in the high mountains. We truly lived a life of freedom, I guess you could call it that. In fact, we worked harder than most people ever did in the settlements and we faced more difficult challenges from weather and Indians and wild animals. You learned a lot about the food chain in your first few weeks there in the wilderness.

A novice mountain man had to realize that the life of animals and the life of humans was all one long, connected chain. As long as you felt that you were empowered by the food chain you are okay. It's just when you began to realize that mountain lions and wolves and grizzly bears and black bears didn't see it that way. In fact, they considered you as part of their food supply, and that gave you a very different perspective regarding the food chain.

Every Mountain Man who came to the rendezvous and who was worth his salt, knew the reality of the food chain. We took advantage of the beaver and harvested their pelts whether they liked it or not! Did that make us important on the food chain? I'm not sure, but it certainly was a stressful way to make a living. It was also very messy, though no one wanted to talk about that.

The difficult life we lead in the mountains seemed to just burst forth and explode when it came time for the rendezvous. It's like each mountain man was sitting on a powder keg of energy and the rendezvous was the fuse. When it was lit, all hell broke loose. I think I can say we had fun at the rendezvous, but it got crazy a lot of the time. The previous year Clyde and I had taken advantage of the drunken mountain men who were fools enough to wager against my skills as a sober member of the competitions.

We weren't sure we could pull it off again this year, but we certainly were going to try. As we rode up to the rendezvous I was very conscious of my wife. The year before, when Clyde and I had attended that first rendezvous there was no wife, there was no Little Fire. It was through the rendezvous that I had met her and if it hadn't been for that meeting we would never have gotten together as man and wife. So in fact, we owed a lot to the rendezvous and this year she wasn't sure how safe she would be with all these crazy and lustful men. The year before she was sheltered by the tribe, her brother, her father, the other Mandan Braves.

Clyde and I had had several conversations about this matter of her safety, before we got to the Popo Agie location. We decided that both of us would have to do our best to stay sober and that at any given time one or the other would be watching my wife. We must never let her out of our sight, because there was a lot of danger everywhere. The danger clearly came from the mountain men who considered Indian women fair game for their sexual needs. There were many stories on the frontier of mountain men abusing physically and sexually Native American women for their satisfaction and the rage that dwelt within them.

This year, there was little or no chance that her tribe would be attending the rendezvous as they had the year before. But there would be other tribes there and that too posed a challenge to our diligence regarding the safety of my wife.

Chapter 35: Rendezvous 1826

I have to say that as we approached the gathering and I saw all the tents and the smells of food being barbecued on the open fires, I could feel my juices flowing. I was excited. My first experience the year before had been one of exhilaration, probably for the most part because I was by and large sober throughout the rendezvous. In talking with the men at Feldman's trading post after the rendezvous, many of them could only remember what happened through a kind of fog. Some of them clearly were still hung over a month later from all the drinking they had done.

The alcohol at the rendezvous was sold out of Bent's Fort or Fort Collins or Jacob Astor's trading post or one that was being started by Jim Bridger, and let me tell you, that alcohol was very dangerous. I'm not sure the damage that it could do to the human body, but from for what I could see, it certainly looked serious enough. At the Collins Trading Post we had purchased a tent, and that would be our home for the rendezvous.

The previous year, the rendezvous had been held at the confluence of the Sandy River and the Green River, but this year it would be held further to the east at a place called Popo Agie, This location was further north and east, almost up into the mountains. As we approached the rendezvous this year we could see all the tents spread out and the herds of horses off to the side. We could distinctly see the main thoroughfare where all the trading posts had set up their goods and where all the beaver trading was being done.

We had gone to Fort Collins for our beaver trading because we felt we could get a better deal, knowing that at the rendezvous, Astor and Ashley and the Bent brothers were paying much lower prices, something they had all agreed on, because they said they were coming out to us and it was costing them! No one believed that, but they had such a solid agreement among themselves that none of the mountain men found a way to break through. And they were literally paying about half of what the pelts were worth.

That's why we were so surprised at Fort Collins to get such good money for our pelts and now looking back in retrospect from the Popo Agie rendezvous, we had certainly done the right thing and it paid off handsomely. As I rode up on my leopard Appaloosa I could hear men commenting on the fact that my horse had been the prize of the rendezvous of eighteen twenty-five. Word had gotten around on the frontier that I was the best shot, the best man with the hatchet, and the best one at throwing a knife, I had been the rendezvous champion!

Clyde had told me that that was going to be so this year when we first arrived. But he also warned me what that meant. It was like having a big target on my forehead because now the others would be trying to take the prize this year and beat me at all the competitions. They had now seen me in action and knew what I could do and this year there would be no fooling, we couldn't take advantage like we did the last time, or so he said.

I countered with the fact that, "They're going to have alcohol again this year aren't they? They're all going to be drunk again this year aren't they? They're all going to want to show that they know a good knife thrower, a good musket man and a good hatchet thrower when they see one won't they?" Clyde couldn't argue with me on that score and as I knew he would be looking to make some money again. I figured I could count on him for a 50-50 split of the proceeds.

I also knew that Clyde had a lot of money, much more than he had the year before because of the sale of our pelts at Fort Collins. I knew he'd be wagering higher than he did the year before and that we stood to earn some serious money. Once we knew that we were going to the rendezvous at Popo Aggie, I began carefully working at my skills with the knife, the hatchet and the musket. I felt that I was still better than most and could hold my own against the likes of hatchet Jack, Bill Tyler, and big Bill Davis! Time would tell.

Chapter 36: Popo Agie

We had agreed that we would head right into camp at the rendezvous with my leopard Appaloosa leading the way. I smiled at Clyde's ability for self-promotion, but I agreed with him that it would be a good way to boost our standings when it came to the competitions of the tournament. There was an area set up for tents for the mountain men and it was on the far side of the main thoroughfare. We had to ride right through and this year I was proud to ride my Appaloosa with the fine new saddle, knowing that right behind me was my beautiful Indian wife who also drew a lot of attention, I might add.

We headed directly for the area where the tents were being set up for the mountain men and took a place there unfastening our packs and putting down the tent. We set it up in no time, the three of us had gotten really good at doing that already, and we organized our bedding as we usually did, though Clyde frequently chose to sleep outside the tent, giving us some privacy.

In no time at all we were surrounded by friends from the year before and there was a lot of backslapping and catching up on the news of the previous year. Most mountain men already knew that we had spent the winter with the Mandans on the Missouri River, and that the Mandan camp had been abandoned in early spring because of the smallpox outbreak.

That had been two months before and so they could easily see that the three of us were clear of any symptoms and accepted our assurances that we had never shown any signs of the disease. The mountain men had come to know Rolling Thunder and Little Hawk from the year before and were concerned about their welfare. My wife continued her silent role of arranging our belongings inside the tent and made no appearance among the mountain men though I could see several of them trying to get a glance at her inside the tent.

I realized that our apprehensions were well-founded and we would have to be careful for her safety during the rendezvous. These men of the mountains were not easily deterred from what they desired or wanted or thought they desired or wanted. Add the element of alcohol to that and you had real trouble.

There were many questions about whether I would join in the competitions this year and I assured them that I would. I knew that word of my challenge would circulate within the hour among the rendezvous participants. They had also heard of my conflict with the Blackfeet and the killing of Running Wolf and his brother Eagle's Wing. I have to admit that I was startled by the fact that they were so well-informed about my life! News traveled fast on the frontier as I come to learn.

It was always amazing whenever you ran into someone on the trail or when someone came to visit an Indian tribe like the Mandan, almost immediately news was conveyed from the frontier south and north, east and west, there were very few limits to the flow of information. I could barely remember what it was like back in the settlements on the other side of the Mississippi and the Missouri where people actually read newspapers! On the frontier you didn't need a newspaper to catch up on the information and the events going on throughout the mountains. You just listened to travelers and around campfires, you got all the news.

It was getting close to suppertime now and the three of us went over to the food tent where biscuits and beef stew had been prepared for the evening meal. There was even chicken if you wanted to spend the money and I was feeling very generous at that point. Little Fire and I purchased half a chicken which we both enjoyed thoroughly and devoured completely for our dinner that evening. The noise and raucous laughter of the food tent was a little bit too much for us and so we quickly ate our supper and left Clyde there with his friends to go out and walk along the river.

We had a lot to talk about because the rendezvous brought back memories to both of us. The Green River rendezvous is where we had met and we talked about that and about how generous her family was in taking me in for the winter. Though she didn't need to hear it, I reiterated my admiration and my gratitude for her father and what he had done for me last year. I told her how much I cared about her brother Little Hawk, and hoped we would be able to visit them again soon this year. We sat by the river and held one another as the sun was going down over the mountains to the west. It was good time for us to be together.

Chapter 37: Tournament Time

The previous year I had been a surprise entry in the tournaments at the rendezvous. I believe that I was able to take advantage of three well-established champions because they didn't see me coming. Both Clyde and I knew that this year it was not going to be the same and I think those we had taken advantage of knew how we had tricked them. Not that my skill itself was not genuine, because I had to hit the target like anyone else, but alcohol did play a part both in my winning and in the betting that was done on my behalf.

Clyde had taken advantage of the fact that most the mountain men were drunk and wouldn't remember the bets they had made the next day. The life of the wilderness was strange in that way, once or twice a year you had more money in your pocket than you could imagine, the rendezvous was one of those times. Wagering came easy to men who hardly understood what it meant to lose hard earned money that fast.

We came away with quite a bit of money as a result of all this wagering, drunken as it may have been. Things would be different this year because people would be on the lookout for the two of us and what some mountain men had begun to call our "wagering scheme." What it was, in my opinion, was a really smart man, Clyde Patterson, taking advantage of a situation!

Because I was the current champion of the tournaments, everyone wanted to be sure that I was matched up against the best man at the rendezvous. Jacob Astor was there again as was Gen. Ashley and now the Bent brothers also wanted in on the activities of the tournament. Naturally the tournament activities brought a lot of attention to those who were selling weapons and even trapper utensils like knives and hatchets. One of the Bent brothers even came up to me and asked if I would use one of their hatchets in the contest! Now I was part of their marketing!

I really loved the location of this year's rendezvous and my wife and I took advantage of the waterfalls and the beautiful mountain views of the wilderness. I was happy to spend time with her walking the rivers and sitting by the waterfalls, we had many pleasant talks during that time. This year Clyde and I were not trading beaver pelts because of our previous arrangement at Fort Collins, so Little Fire and I had more time to spend together and wander about the different stalls where traders were hawking their goods.

One of the things that I had wanted to buy her was a musket, because I wanted her to have an opportunity to learn to fire a weapon for self-protection. We spent a lot of time in the various booths that were selling pistols and rifles, I wanted something that would be light enough for her to handle easily, but accurate enough for her to become good and skilled with firearms. Fortunately I had plenty of money to spend this time around and there were plenty of opportunities for us to replenish our supplies of food for the road ahead.

I managed to procure for my wife an excellent knife that would serve her for the work that we had to do skinning and butchering beaver but at the same time be a good weapon for self-defense if she needed it. The pistol that we bought was also very well-made and light to handle, and to my surprise, I should've known better since she was a war chief's daughter, she took to both weapons with her usual enthusiasm. Because there was a lot of ammunition available at the rendezvous, we took a lot of time outside the camp to practice with her two guns and in no time at all she was doing very well with both the pistol and the rifle.

I'd purchased a hatchet for her as well and then while I was practicing for my own tournament activities, she began practicing as well right alongside me. She quickly learned the skill of throwing the balanced hatchet and in no time at all she was competing with me! I couldn't believe it! I was supposed to be the best one at the rendezvous, and here she was giving me a good run for my money.

It was gratifying to know that she soon would be able to defend herself using these weapons and it gave me comfort to know that she would be more safe because of them. As far as the tournament competitions went, I felt that I was ready and told my partner so. He explained to me that the competition was going to be different this year, that Hatchet Jack was not even at the rendezvous and that my competition would be a half breed called Johnny Rainwater. Clyde said to be careful with that one because word was that the man never drank alcohol! Apparently, Bill Tyler had also been injured in an avalanche down in the Gallatins, and he wouldn't be here either!

Chapter 38: Crooked Nose

It was time for the tournament and without Hatchet Jack, things seemed more disorganized than ever. William Bent, the trader, seemed to want to take charge of the situation and began by asking who was last year's champion, to which I responded, "That would be me, Sam Ogden!"

"Anyone want to challenge the rendezvous champion?" Bent shouted trying to get the attention of the boisterous crowd of mountain men and Indians. This year there seem to be a much greater number of Indians from the various tribes and now I could tell that they represented Crow and Blackfeet and even Comanche and Lakota. I have to say that the Comanche looked at me rather strange and in their own angry way, probably wanted to take my scalp as I had been known along the frontier to have escaped their clutches once already!

"I'll take him on, that young greenhorn, Hatchet Jack's a good friend of mine, he would've won last year I'll tell you, if he hadn't had so much of that damn good Kentucky whiskey," the man shouted to the laughter of the already drunk group of mountain men.

I looked over at my adversary and saw an older mountain man who went by the name of Crooked Nose. The way he was slurring his words made me think that there wouldn't be much competition coming from him.

This year they had set up a chunk of log about two feet long on a barrel so that the butt end of the log stuck out as the target face. It was pine and it took the hatchets pretty well. I tried it a few times already and found it to be a decent target. As always there were three black rings, one right around the outer edge, one half way to the middle and one in the center about the width of a man's hand.

As usual, we were each given three throws and allowed to choose the best of the three as our entry in the competition. My challenger went first since it was up to him to prove that he was better than me. Crooked Nose did a fairly good imitation of Hatchet Jack and I had to smile remembering my competition with the renowned Mountain Man from the previous year.

The older mountain man pulled up a sprig of grass and threw it in the air and it dropped right where he threw it, as there was no wind at all this day. That brought plenty of laughter from the crowd and then he did his imitation of Hatchet Jack looking at the target across the back edge of the hatchet as though he were sighting a rifle. That too brought a lot of laughter from the crowd as they all knew Hatchet Jack's style and his mannerisms.

The first hatchet throw struck about halfway in and the attendant pulled the hatchet out and handed it back to Crooked Nose who threw again, but with less attention and the blade of the hatchet caught the outer edge of the stump and flew off to the side almost injuring one of the Indians standing nearby. The third throw of the hatchet was not better than the first and therefore William Bent went up to the target stump and drew an X with charcoal at the spot where Crooked Nose had hit the target.

I lined up for my first throw and to my surprise struck exactly at the spot where Crooked Nose had made his best throw. Everyone laughed at that because after all what were the odds of that happening? My second throw cheated in just a little bit from the mark left by Crooked Nose, so I had already won the competition but I had a third throw to go anyway so I took it. It struck dead center and everyone started jumping up and down.

Backing me up in his own way, Clyde Patterson had made sure that bets were laid, some of the mountain men choosing the seasoned veteran and others putting the money on last year's champion, me. Clyde whispered to me that he cleared fifteen dollars on that bet, so we were off to a good start!

Chapter 39: Johnny Hatchetman

Now a cry rose up from among the Indians who were there. I noticed especially the Crow members of the gathering were shouting loudest. They wanted to see how I could do against the half breed Johnny Rainwater. Even though they were generally not partial to half breeds, Johnny seemed to be a favorite among most of the Indians. He looked like them and he dressed like them, they wanted to see him go up against last year's champion.

Johnny insisted that I go first, wanting to have the advantage of knowing what he was up against and I agreed to that. I could've probably insisted to go second but the Indians seem pretty stirred up about getting their man to win. I stepped up to the throwing line at about forty feet from the large round target and threw my first hatchet, landing it about an inch from the center on the right side. The second throw landed on the left side just about the same distance from the center I felt good about putting that third hatchet right down the middle and that's what happened, my third throw struck dead center.

I stepped back and nodded to my adversary and said, "Let's see what you can do Johnny Hatchet Man!" That drew some laughter from the crowd though most of the Indians obviously didn't understand what I said. There was a moment of silence on their part because of that. Johnny stepped up to the throwing line and made his first toss. He missed the center by about eight inches and I could see that he felt the pressure and the expectation of the Indians. He was a wiry man, about thirty-five years old, it was clear he had seen some hard living in the mountains.

Having been raised in an Indian village, Johnny had been throwing Tomahawks since he was five years old. The tomahawk that he had was hatchet shaped, and like many of the Indians he used not a stone hatchet but instead a steelhead like the one that I used. The difference was that his hatchet was much lighter than mine probably almost half a pound lighter I would say, and the head was much smaller. You could argue in both directions for why a lighter hatchet was easier to throw or more accurate, but I preferred my hatchet to the tomahawk style.

Johnny's second throw was four inches closer to the center and now he was down to his last turn. The silence came over the gathering at that moment and the men pushed back to give him room and in a graceful motion he pulled back with his tomahawk and threw very intently. He missed the center by about an inch, may be a little bit less, but clearly less than mine, which meant that once again I had won the hatchet throw. This year I chose to take the ten dollar prize as the winner, saying to William Bent and to those who had organized the tournament that I hoped that Hatchet Jack would be back next year and I was looking forward to meeting up with him again.

As we walked away from the hatchet throwing competition, Clyde said to me that he had made another twenty dollars in cash and took payment of three good hunting knives off of several Sioux warriors who were there. We had had a good night.

Chapter 40: Knife Throwing

Big Bill Davis had arrived about midmorning the next day. As it turned out, he was just in time for the knife throwing competition at which he excelled. Davis had come near to getting scalped the previous week by a band of Blackfoot he ran into up on the Wind River Range. He was still cussing at that particular band of Indians and when he saw me he said, "I thought you had finished up them Blackfeet the summer before. Heard you'd gotten into a great skirmish with Running Wolf and done them in good and proper!" The big man said as he wrapped me in a bear hug.

"We took care of business, what did you expect? Saved old Feldman a lot of grief, I'd wager!" I responded.

"I suspect you're ready to take me on this year, throwing that knife or yours, or you going to chicken out on me?" He said with his usual dancing eyes. I could never forget the way his eyes seemed to sparkle and shine, something real unusual.

"I'll be there, you can count on it, but I lost my knife in a skirmish with the Lakota up on the Missouri last winter The new one I got just ain't the same. Holds an edge fine but balance is not perfect, not the way I like it anyway," I replied. Clyde had put a lot of work into that old knife, and damn the balance was just the way I liked it. Somehow it got lost in the night attack that we did with the Mandans against the Lakotas.

That afternoon William Bent came up to me and said, "Davis assured me that he would not join in the competition unless you were part of it, said he felt you cheated him last year, don't know what he meant by that!" Bent said looking at me kind of funny.

"I don't know what Davis meant by that sir, but you can count on me as part of the competition, always glad to join in!" I replied. Clyde Patterson was standing next to me and he nudged me with his arm and winked. Clyde was the only one who knew about the knife situation that I was in and I think somehow he knew that my skill with the new knife was not the same as it had been the year before.

We all gathered at the knife throwing range and it was determined that all throwing this year would be done from thirty-five feet. I could see that Joe Walker was there in the crowd but he had chosen not to compete this year after his humiliation by Big Bill Davis the year before. Joe and Big Bill had an ongoing argument over who was the better knife thrower for almost two years before Davis finally whipped him good and proper at the rendezvous of eighteen twenty-five.

This year there were a couple of new entries, men that I never met before. One of them was a legend among mountain men, his name was Jedediah Smith and he was indeed a grizzled veteran. Clyde had told me that whenever

Smith was at a rendezvous he always participated in the knife throwing, thought he was good with the knife, though everyone knew he wasn't. There were two other men who had joined in the competition this year that I had seen briefly at Feldman's trading post, Jeremiah Wilson and Josh McTaggart. Both of them were pretty well liquored up by the time it came to throwing knives that afternoon and I could see that they weren't taking the competition seriously.

My first competition was with McTaggart and I let him go first as he seemed eager to get started. His first throw missed the target completely and everyone howled with laughter, McTaggart included. His second throw came in about six inches from center, so I knew that I was up against a serious knife thrower. But then his third throw held at about the same distance from the center on the opposite side and that was about the best he could do.

I stepped to the throwing line and my first throw came in at about the same distance as McTaggart's, six inches below the center. I was surprised that the knife had gone so low, I wasn't expecting that. Like the day before, there was literally no wind to factor in. The good thing was that I knew I was right on target with my alignment. My second throw came in about three inches from the center so I'd already won the contest but chose to do the third throw anyway. Clyde insisted that I do that as part of my adjustment to that day's throwing.

My third throw stuck the edge of the center circle which was about an inch across, still nowhere near a perfect throw, but close enough to take that round.

Chapter 41: Jedediah Smith

Smith had beat the man they call Jay Wilson, shortened for his given name of Jeremiah. Clyde told me that their competition had been pretty fierce and that both men had broken the center circle, though Smith's throw was the more accurate of the two. I was surprised at that because it seemed to me that Wilson was pretty well liquored up. I didn't see the same with Jedediah Smith.

He was well known as one of the first men into the mountains after the Lewis and Clark expedition. He was already leading caravans of supply wagons and even one or two that were wagon trains on the southern route toward Santa Fe. Smith had let it be known that he wasn't much interested in trapping, said he thought it was a vile trade and couldn't understand why people wanted to buy beaver pelts and make hats out of them. But he did love the rendezvous, loved to be around people and loved to spend money. He also liked his Kentucky whiskey.

I could smell the liquor on his breath as he pushed ahead of me to the throwing line. He use the old expression, "age before beauty," and everyone got a laugh out of that one. I have to admit he was good with the knife and each of his throws clustered in around the center ring, but he only broke it once on the left side, not a direct hit at all.

When my turn came I stood at the line and my first throw came in just below the center circle. I was obviously hitting on a perfect alignment that day since my other throws had gone in a vertical direction as well. I looked hard at the center of the target for my second throw and the blade of the knife broke the ring but not much closer than Smith's had been. My final throw hit dead center and that was what I needed to take the second round and move on to face big Bill Davis.

Davis had dispatched his competition with ease, but he got a good run for his money from a half breed, a nasty looking man they called Hickory Tom. The man was well-built and very dark complexioned, showing his Indian blood. His mother had been a Cherokee, I was told, and his father had been an English trader. What was impressive about the man was that he seemed to be all muscle and he moved with a grace and fluidity that made you think of a mountain lion. His eyes were black and when he smiled it seemed as though he had a plan to kill you.

I don't think I ever felt that way about another human being, but Hickory Tom seemed like just a real mean sonofabitch. Even Big Bill Davis was subdued in the presence of this half breed. The man could use a knife however, and he put two throws in the center ring one of which struck dead center. Davis was going to have to match that in order to go on to another throw off. I was surprised to see Davis struggle with the situation, he seemed intimidated by the half breed.

Finally, his third throw struck center exactly where Hickory Tom's knife had landed, on his final throw. They went to a second round and this time the half breed missed the center by almost a half an inch. Davis knew he had to hit dead center in order to win the match, and effectively he did. William Bent announced that there would be a pause now in the competition and we would all come back in an hour to complete the knife throwing event, which he called "The match of champions!"

I know what he meant by that since Davis had been the champion before me and I was the champion from eighteen twenty-five. It did sound a little pretentious but, hell, the buzz was out and everybody who had been sitting around drinking and doing nothing, decided they wanted to see the two champions go at one another. Bill Davis thrived on that kind of attention, but I'm not sure that I did. It was then more than ever that I was missing my favorite knife, the one that Clyde had made for me.

Chapter 42: Match of Champions!

There was still a lot of daylight left that afternoon as we stood at the knife throwing line and prepared for what would be the final match of the day. I watched as Big Bill took a good swig of Kentucky whiskey and wiped his mouth on the sleeve of his buckskin shirt. "You ready for this boy, still don't know how you beat me last year, God dammit! You goin' to get spanked this time, that's for sure," the big man shouted.

As usual, he insisted that I go first, and because he was the senior member and had been champion for two years before me, I took my throws as he requested. For some reason that day I was in this vertical thing, I guess, because my knife throws went from two inches below center to one inch below center, to probably about a quarter of an inch below center, well inside the one inch round circle. Those attending the competition let out a sigh of admiration for what I had just done. I'd set the bar pretty high for Big Bill Davis but I knew he was more than capable of meeting the challenge.

As he strode up to the line with his usual air of confidence and swagger, he said to me in a soft voice, "That all you got boy?" And I knew I was in trouble.

To prove he was the undisputed champion, Davis did exactly the same thing I did going from right to left, toward the center. The first throw was two inches out, second throw one inch out, and by dammit, the third throw hit dead center, he had beat me!

A roar went up from the crowd and I expected my partner Clyde would be upset with me because we had lost in the wagering department. However, clever as usual, Clyde at taken odds on both of us and as it turned out he not only broke even on that one, but came out ahead by ten or fifteen dollars! I said to him, "You are conniving sonofabitch aren't you?" He just smiled and turned both hands upward as though to say, "What are you gonna do when you're as good as I am!" We both got a good laugh out of that one and I was no longer champion.

Clyde's response to the situation was that he would make me a better knife next year, and we'd be back. During the competitions we had made sure that Little Fire spent the evening or the afternoon with friends of hers from the Hidatsa tribe who were attending the rendezvous. If I understand correctly they were distant relatives of some kind, I'm not sure Indians ever talked about cousins but I think it was something like that. She seemed very happy with the time she was spending there when we went to get her.

She could tell however from the look on my face that I had not won the competition this time and she said to me, "You know it's okay with me if you're not the champion!" And she had a mystifying smile on her face as she said that, I'm not too sure what she meant. Clyde went over to join some of the mountain men for a drink of whiskey, and Little Fire and I went for a walk along the river and up to the falls.

It was a beautiful moonlit night and so we enjoyed the sound of the water as it glistened in the white light of the moon. She seemed happy with the time that she had spent there among the Hidatsa. They were her people and she had gotten some news about her family and found that they were doing well and no further losses had happened from the smallpox after their move west of the Missouri. She asked me how long we were going to be at the rendezvous and what we would be doing next and we talked about what she would like to do. Clyde and I knew that it was our intention to head south toward the Bent's trading post on the Arkansas River.

From there, we would head up into the Gallatins for our winter cabin. For her, this was all new territory and she said she looked forward to seeing the southern mountains. I admired her freedom and her commitment to our marriage. I know that if she had insisted that we stay with her family at the Mandan Village, I would probably still be there. We were partners in life now.

Chapter 43: Rifle Competition

Last year, at the Green River rendezvous, the rifle competition ended up with Jim Tyler and myself in the final round. Tyler's magnificent Hawken rifle, every bit a fifty caliber, misfired on the third shot in the second time we went around. The rules of the competition were so loose that anything could disqualify a contestant, even a gun misfiring and so I won, and for a year I was the champion!

Several times I'd heard men grumbling about the way I won the championship. The first time occurred at the Feldman trading post after we'd gotten a little bit liquored up. This year would be a chance for me to prove that I was indeed the champion. My fifty caliber Hawken was now battle tested after the skirmishes we had with the Blackfeet at the Feldman trading post and everyone knew about it.

When it was finally time for the competition and I arrived at the firing range, several men came up to me and asked to hold the Hawken. They wanted to see how it was weighted and balanced. I enjoyed the feeling of celebrity at that moment, though I was not quite sure that they were rooting for me when it came to the competition that evening.

The sun was already setting when they began to set up the targets and the first rounds were taken. Because I was champion from the previous year, I got a pass on the first rounds and three pairs of shooters had already gone before me when I finally stepped to the line. I was surprised to see Joe Walker back again for another go with the rifles, though I knew his reputation as a long shooter. The first round, the targets had been set at 100 feet and now for the second round they had been moved back twenty-five, making it a little bit more difficult.

The range of the Hawken rifle was obviously at least three times that, especially the fifty caliber. This time Joe Walker nodded to me and it was gratifying to hear him say my name as he got set for his first round against me. He had easily won the first series against a younger shooter and said he was eager to match bullets with me. After his defeat of eighteen twenty-five, Jim Tyler had chosen not to even come to the rendezvous this year and like Hatchet Jack he was missed by the men attending.

Walker was shooting a forty caliber Hawken and his first shot at the frying pan was spectacular. They had hung the frying pan on a rope off a tree branch next to the table where the other two targets were resting. When the Hawken ball hit the frying pan it spun and then flipped up over the branch and several men standing around said they were sure the tree was shaking. I can't be sure that was true, but the way that frying pan spun was quite a show.

Walker easily dispatched the small pot. The metal pot went flying off the table and seemed to hang in the air before it went thudding to the ground behind the table. There was still good light coming off a late sunset and the Beacon fires had been built next to the table were beginning to shed some light, and the torches that were standing near the table, gave a good light as well. There were no shadows on the little tin cup as it sat and sparkled in the evening firelight. Joe Walker gave it a good shot, though it wasn't a clean shot and it looked as though he caught the thumb handle of the cup, because it spun away off to the side clearing the table as required.

As Joe Walker stepped back from the shooting line I could hear him mumbling to himself, "God damn luck on that one!" He said in a soft voice and I could see a small wry smile cross his lips. It took a few moments for them to get the targets reset as we were just in the second round and now it was my turn.

My first shot took the frying pan dead center and there was a ringing sound that seemed to echo across the river, a deep resounding gong almost. I quickly reloaded and got set for the first shot on the table, the small pot that had taken the place of the one Joe Walker had destroyed. There was a bit of flickering to the light and some shadows now, because the sun had completely dipped down below the horizon and dusk was beginning to spread over the river.

My second shot hit the pot dead center and you could see fragments flying in all directions as the pot toppled off the back of the table, sliding first across the wood surface. Now for the final and most difficult shot of all, the tin cup. If I made this shot, then Joe Walker and I would do another round. I knew Joe Walker had been lucky when he hit the tin cup on the edge of the handle and I wondered if there was some problem with the wind or the angle or something like that. I chose to compensate just in case, shooting just a fraction to the left of center on the cup and my ball went true, driving the cup off into the night air behind the table. We would now be on to a second round. I was feeling good about the Hawken that night. I wondered if Joe Walker was actually feeling lucky!

Chapter 44: Second Time Around

The way the rules had been set up for the shooting competition, a second round required that the targets be moved back another twenty-five feet. That meant we were now shooting at 150 feet and neither Joe Walker nor myself saw that as a problem. Walker was known for his long vision, that was well known on the frontier. Mountain Men spoke of his unerring accuracy whenever they got into skirmishes with Indians. Joe Walker was always the one they called on to take the long distance kill shot on an enemy.

This time the frying pan would be set up on the table leaning against a block of wood. The target was designed in such a way that the wood was not attached to the table and when the bullet struck, it would carry both the pan and the wood backwards off the table. Joe and I both agreed to this design which was supposed to prevent a bullet from going ricochet into the crowd.

Once again a large number of mountain men had gathered around the shooting line where we stood to take aim. My partner Clyde Patterson was busy laying bets and since the first round against Walker had not produced a winner, the wagering got higher the second time around. Walker was a seasoned mountain man, one of the originals as I heard tell, and he was probably not going to make the same mistake Jim Tyler made the year before, causing his rifle to misfire.

Once again Joe Walker went first taking his three shots at the targets now sitting on the heavy table at the end of the shooting range. All the lighting now was coming from the bonfires on either side of the table and torches that had been set up closer to the table itself. Everyone in attendance could see clearly the three target and Joe began as before with the frying pan which he struck full center pushing it back to the edge of the table where it teetered for a while and then dropped off the back side.

The crowd made a funny sound at that point almost like a sigh, as many of them had put some serious money on the expertise of Joe Walker with the rifle. Joe had one shot at the second target and this time his bullet only grazed the metal pot, causing it to slide slightly to the left but not leave the table. You could hear a loud moan from the crowd as those wagering on Joe Walker could feel their hard-earned pelt money slipping away.

I have to give it to Joe Walker, he really did bounce back when it came to that final shot! He must've compensated slightly because this time his ball took the tin cup dead center and sent it flying into the darkness behind the table. Now it was my turn to put an end to this round of shooting and I began by first knocking the frying pan clean off the table, wood block and all. I'd seen from the way Joe Walker's shot had taken the frying pan and knew that you had to hit it just below center and not dead center. I suspect it's because the sides of the frying pan might've been tapered some but I'm not sure.

This whole round depended on what I could do with that metal pot in the middle of the table since that was where Joe Walker had given me my chance. Once again I noted that he had grazed the pot on the right side, the same mistake he had made with the tin cup hitting it only on the handle in the first round. So again, I compensated by about a half inch and drilled the pot dead center lifting it in the air and everyone could hear it clanging as it hit some rocks behind the table where it landed. This time I could hear those who had wagered on Sam Ogden letting out a sigh of relief and there were a few cheers from the large crowd that had gathered.

After my experience with the small pot I decided to do the same thing again with the tin cup and I was pleased with my results. The tin cup took my shot dead center and pieces of metal flew in all directions as the cup disintegrated and slid backwards off the table. For now, I was headed to the final round and would have my chance to once again be champion of the rendezvous.

Granted, this year I had not been able to win both of the first two competitions, but rifle competition was the supreme test. I had to win, I just had to!

Chapter 45: John Westerly

The other shooting match had also gone into a second round and produced a winner finally, an Englishman named John Westerly. He had come to the Rocky Mountain wilderness in eighteen twenty, according to my partner Clyde Patterson. No one was sure how much trapping he had done as he seemed to favor the larger game and the word was that he had mostly sold buffalo robes with a few wolf pelts mixed in. He was shooting an English-made rifle, that was as long as my Hawken and sure did look fancy with that light-colored stock and engraved metal.

It was said that Westerly had won tournaments in England and that he considered what we did at the rendezvous as well beneath his skill with the rifle. I believe he was surprised by the fact that he was taken to a second round, and it looked as though he found shooting at night to be undignified.

We drew straws to see who would go first and as it turned out I was the one who drew the shorter straw and so I would shoot first in this championship round. It wasn't my favorite way to do things, as I believe that I had taken advantage of Joe Walker already, noticing how his shots were drifting to the right. I guessed that there must've been some kind of a breeze crossing the shooting range that night, it might have been complicated by the intense heat from the fires and the torches.

Before I took my first shot I pulled a few strands of grass and held them up to the wind, and dammit yes there was a wind moving across the field of fire. I would make compensation for that, calibrating my shot to take in the adjustment for the wind. We were shooting at 200 yards for this final round and the fires were dying down some now, so I asked those in attendance to build the fires up and Clyde made sure that that got done, taking away some of the shadows that were dancing on the target table.

My first shot struck the frying pan dead center, flipping it back over the block of wood that was supporting it and dropping it behind the table as was required by the rules. The small pot was a bit more difficult, and my shot wasn't a direct center hit, but the pot went flying off the table anyway. The fact that I hadn't hit the pot dead center concerned me as I lined up my shot for the tin cup, my final target in that round.

Once again I thought about the wind coming across from right to left and adjusted my aim to compensate for that little bit of draft on the part of my bullet. This time, I hit the cup dead center and sent it flying about six feet off the table. The wagering had been fierce before this match as men were taking sides against the English rifle and the Englishman, who always seemed a bit too dainty for the tastes of my fellow mountain men.

A loud shout went up when I hit that final target as the men began to doubt the way the pot had danced off the table as to whether I was losing my edge. John Westerly strode to the line looking at me as though I were unworthy competition for someone of his lofty skills. The gun he was firing was only forty caliber and at 200 feet didn't pack the kick of my fifty caliber weapon. As a result, it looked as though the pan might not even clear the table on that first shot. He had hit it cleanly, you could tell by the way the pan stood on its end and wobble back and forth and then it finally fell off the table! Those whose wager had been in favor of the Englishman, let out a sigh of relief. Their contestant was still in the running.

He did much better with the metal pot which was lighter and he hit it dead center, lifting it clean off the table and dropping it to the ground clattering in the rocks behind the table. I wondered how he would do with the tin cup, as it was a smaller target and once again the fires were going down just a little bit, giving less light and illumination to the target. His bullet did strike cleanly and the tin cup was demolished in the process, we would now go on to the second round.

Chapter 46: Final Pressure

I stood at the firing line with my Hawken resting butt-down on the ground and waited for a nod from my adversary recognizing my turn in the second round of the championship competition. I raised the fifty caliber Hawken to my shoulder and held it tight, once again thinking about the wind which seem to be increasing as the night wore on. I was never quite sure looking back over that moment whether the wind factor was partly due to the large bonfires on either side of the target table, but I had decided that it was a situation that needed adjustment.

I set my aim just a bit to the right of center on the large frying pan hoping it would help me understand the wind factor for the two smaller targets I would be shooting next. We continued at the two hundred foot range as requested by my opponent, who felt that his forty caliber would be at a disadvantage if we extended the target position beyond 200 feet. When the bullet struck the frying pan on that round it set a spark that I could clearly see through the smoke of the musket pan.

The spark told me that indeed my ball had struck dead center on the frying pan and pushed it and the block of wood straight off the back of the table, no hesitation this time. Now I knew when I took aim at the small metal pot that I had to compensate a good half-inch to the right in order to take in the factor of the wind moving across the firing range. My second shot went true and that poor pot would never see the light of day again. The Hawken slug took it out of commission for good. Men still talk about the damage that Hawken did to a fine pot!

The metal cup was next, and now that I knew pretty exactly what the wind was doing there at the target table, the cup was no competition. The fifty caliber Hawken destroyed the cup as well, to the great satisfaction of those men who had wagered on champion Sam Ogden!

As I watched Westerly move to the firing line I could see that he did not have the assurance he had the first time around. He turned to me and nodded for my approval that he should begin and we made eye contact, something that told me he was getting concerned. From his previous round he knew that hitting that frying pan properly was going to make all the difference, he just wasn't sure what properly meant, I could tell by the look in his eyes.

To my surprise, he chose to go in the opposite direction, something I had not seen at all in any of the competitions so far. He called the cup first and said he was going to shoot the tin cup with his first shot, and damn, he hit it clean, the cup went sailing. His bullet on the second pot, the second target, was not quite as clean but the pot finally gave up the ghost and fell off the table dancing a little bit after being struck just off center by the Englishman's ball.

Everyone knew that the real test was now about to happen, whether the forty caliber English rifle could take out the frying pan which we all knew was a heavy sonofabitch. I don't believe the Englishman knew what he needed to do to take out that frying pan, though I thought he had clearly agreed to the way we had set up the wooden block in support of that heavy pan. Whatever the reason, his bullet struck the pan clean but instead of pushing it back like it was supposed to, it just flipped the pan up over on top of the wooden block and left it sitting there rocking back and forth.

Now mind you, the Englishman knew he had hit the target! But he also knew he hadn't fulfilled the requirement which clearly said the target must be knocked off the table if it was sitting on the table. That meant, that I was the winner! I could hear Westerly cursing under his breath at the lowlife tournament rules set up for this shooting match! Anyway I got the twenty-five dollar prize and of course Jacob Astor was there telling everyone again this year that I purchased my Hawken at his trading post in the Arkansas River Valley!

Chapter 47: Winners All

About a dozen men stood around me that night congratulating me for what I had accomplished again this year, winning the shooting contest for the second year in a row. They all wanted to see the Hawken up close and were completely amazed at how heavy it was and the length of the barrel. I kept answering questions like, "It's a genuine Hawken, fifty caliber, by God, now ain't it?" I laughed as I told them yes indeed it was a fifty caliber Hawken and yes indeed I did purchase it at Jacob Astor's trading post in the Arkansas River Valley.

Then one of the men asked me point blank, "Is this here the rifle that killed the war chief of the Blackfeet, Running Wolf?"

I looked the man in the eye and for just a moment the whole scene flashed before my mind as we struggled that day to defend Feldman's Trading Post against the attack by the Blackfoot war party. "My friend, this is indeed the rifle that killed Chief Running Wolf just last summer at the Feldman Trading Post! In fact, it took two bullets from this rifle, dead center in his chest to kill that man! When the first bullet struck him he stopped and stood looking up to the sky as though somehow he had been betrayed by the spirits of his people. I reloaded as fast as I could and he began to move toward me again when he took the second shot also in the center of his chest. That one finally put him down!"

"You don't say! Now by God, that is a hell of a story, young man. I met Chief Running Wolf at Fort Hall several years ago and of all the Indians I ever met I said to myself, that one is destined to be great! When you looked him in the eye, those black eyes of his were as evil as Satan's whelp, I swear to God," the man said and I could hear from the men around us that they were equally impressed.

Things broke up slowly after that with the men going off to their drinking parties and some off to grab a cup of coffee at the mess hall tent. Once the group had cleared away Clyde Patterson came up to me and said, "You thought we were rich last year, by God, you ain't seen nothing yet, my man!" He held out two fistfuls of paper money and a bag of gold coins to make his point.

We were both smiling when we went back to gather up Little Fire from her visit with her friends. It was still early that evening so once again we chose to walk down by the river and she asked me how soon we would be leaving now that the competitions were over. I said we'd leave on the second day, give it one more day, I said, and she was happy for that because she wanted to do a little bit of a wash of some of her particulars. She said that with a little giggle and I didn't even ask what that meant!

I knew I was doing something that meant more to me than spending time drinking with the mountain men as my friend Clyde was doing that night. We got back to our tent and our bedding and made love that night in the privacy of our tent, it felt good, it felt tender, it felt real, God damn I loved that woman so much! We slept in that morning after the tournament and Clyde and I headed over to the mess hall tent with Little Fire trailing behind us. She had brought a bucket with her and after we ate, Clyde and I sat drinking our coffee and she motioned with the bucket that she was going down to the river to get water for the washing she had talked about.

I felt that in broad daylight she would be safe since she was really just going down to the river to get water and come right back. It'd been a hectic few days there at the rendezvous and I was beginning to get tired of all the noise and chatter that was going on around us. Clyde had been up early and was counting our money out so that we could each take our split of the winnings and head out the next morning at sunrise. The year before we had taken almost 500 dollars and this year it was six hundred. I was delighted for the windfall. Little Fire and I could use the three hundred dollars for a nest egg on top of the money we had already made for our pelts that year.

Chapter 48: Trouble at the River

There was so much noise and talking and laughter going on around the mess hall tent that morning that it would've been easy to not hear the screams coming from the river. But then I would've had to been deaf to not hear the scream coming from my wife down at the river bank. I motioned to Clyde and we both heard the scream and where it was coming from and both of us were up in a flash knocking the table over as we ran from the tent.

I carried my rifle with me to breakfast that morning, probably as much out of fear that it might be stolen as anything else. Usually I didn't carry the rifle around camp like that, but this was different, my Hawken had just become the Championship Rifle of the rendezvous. Any thief worth his salt, would go after such a trophy and try to sell it somewhere on the frontier.

I'm not sure how long it took us to reach the bank of the river because it really wasn't that far, but as we crested the high riverbank and look down below to the shoreline we could see immediately what was happening. There were four men gathered around a woman who was lying on the ground, and that woman was by wife! Things happened in a blur as Clyde and I were moving at a full run. I remember that I had my rifle in my hands as we approached the small group.

Two men were standing and two men were kneeling over the woman who was screaming as loud as she could. There was so much racket and noise and laughter and talking going on around the encampment that it was very easy not to hear the scream of someone who was being violated and victimized. I didn't have time to calculate who these four men were but I could tell exactly what they were doing.

One man was kneeling holding her shoulders down as she swung her head from side to side trying to bite if she could the hands that were holding her shoulders. The man kneeling at her feet had spread her legs and torn her buckskin dress up the middle exposing her nakedness and he was now fumbling with his trousers to release his swollen organ for the rape that he had in mind. The other two men were standing alongside the woman's body undoing their trousers in the hopes of taking part in the rape of one more Native American woman.

From the way this was taking place, these men had done it before but they hadn't calculated who this was that they were taking advantage of. For them, it was just a crime of opportunity and in their mind not a crime at all. Native women were the right and privilege of the conquering white men who were taking over the entire country where the Indians had roamed free for hundreds of years.

I came running at the group from behind the one who had spread my wife's legs and was getting ready to rape her. The butt of my rifle struck him in the back of the head so hard that he literally flew off to the left bumping against one of the men standing on that side and I gathered myself to swing at the other man who was holding Little Fire down. He took the heavy butt of the rifle straight in the face and I could hear his nose crunching and blood spurted from his snarling face. Since the man on the left was down, Clyde had taken his hatchet to the man on the right and struck him in the upper arm with the business end of the blade as Clyde called it.

Now these four had been turned into prey and the one man who was still uninjured of the four had pulled his knife on Clyde and was coming at him swinging the blade and shouting, "What the hell, what the hell!" Clyde swung the axe and literally almost cut the man's hand right off where he was holding the knife. You never heard a yell like that before in your whole life, the scream of shock and pain was so intense! The blood spurting from his wrist was covering his whole pant leg now and running down the side of his leg.

The two men that Clyde had injured with the hatchet were now running up the bank and trying to escape while the other two that I had hit with the butt of the rifle were lying and moaning, on the ground, I'm not sure if they were even conscious. None of that meant anything to me at that moment as I gathered Little Fire into my arms and covered her with my jacket. She was whimpering and shaking and I could feel her breath coming rough bursts, as though she were trying to get her breathing back.

I've never seen anyone so frightened as my wife was at that moment. Her eyes couldn't focus, they seem distended and I'm not even sure she recognized who I was, but she clung to me as though she were drowning at sea. It took almost five minutes for her to regain some sense of where she was and what had happened. She kept saying my name over and over again in that wonderful accent of hers, a sound that had become so precious to me! I felt relieved because I could see that she was not physically injured.

Chapter 49: Healing Time

I gathered her up in my arms and carried her up the bank toward our tent which was just a few hundred yards from where the attack had taken place. What had happened that morning was the one thing I had dreaded and that we hoped to have prevented by watching over her as carefully as we did. It was not enough.

Clyde accompanied me back to our tent and we did our best to calm down the frightened woman, my wife, the dearest person to me in the whole world. In a matter of minutes I'd almost lost the only thing that mattered to me in the whole world. I knew it, she knew it, and Clyde knew it. Those four men were still alive and the only reason they were, is that Clyde and I got in there in time. Those sorry sons of bitches would've been dead already, all four them if it hadn't been for the fact that my wife had survived the attack and caring for her right then was all that mattered.

It seemed like a very long time that I held her there on our bedroll in the tent and things had gotten very quiet outside as word of this thing got around very quickly. Jacob Astor and General Ashley were at the door of our tent along with William Bent, and Clyde was talking with them in a quiet voice. The one thing I heard him say was this, "You'd better make sure that those four men are long gone, because when Sam comes out of this, no one can guarantee their safety!" The traders knew exactly what my friend was saying and they hurried out to take care of this task.

For me right now, all I wanted to do was to comfort and console this bright and lovely young woman who had become the center of my universe. After a while her breathing came back to normal and the shuddering and the shaking that she had been going through gradually subsided. To my surprise, she fell asleep as I held her there in the comforts of our Buffalo robes and for just a moment I was able to regain some focus myself. I had been through a lot since coming to the wilderness, a grisly bear attack, an Indian attack, being captured by the Comanches, hand to hand combat with Eagle's Wing.

I thought I'd seen it all, but nothing compared at all to what had happened today, not even close! A gnawing feeling of helplessness came over me, knowing that I had not prevented this from happening to her no matter how hard I tried! I watched her sleeping profoundly and every once in a while she would shake and let out little sounds that must've been her mind and body reliving the trauma of that moment. I couldn't imagine my life without her, if something like that had happened, it would be such a terrible thing that I could probably never recuperate or recover.

For now, I just wanted her to rest and sleep and I kept stroking her face gently with my hand. I wanted to make it all better, but I knew I couldn't. I could never make up to her for what had just happened. No amount of revenge or retaliation against those stupid lowlifes could ever change what happened to my Little Fire. Then her friends, the

Hidatsas came, two women who knew her well, and were somehow even related, were now at the door of the tent asking for her.

Clyde knew right away who they were and in fact I believe he was the one who had summoned them to come and help us at this time. They found me sitting, cradling her body and her mind, and they sat down on the ground near our bed and said nothing. There was nothing to be said, we knew it, we all knew it, but thankfully Little Fire would heal. They already knew what had happened and why it happened and how it happened. These were women of the frontier, they understood the terrible realities that went on throughout the Rocky Mountains.

We all sat there for probably a good hour before Little Fire finally came around and woke, and recognized me and her two friends. She somehow knew what had happened to the men who had tried to rape her. She knew that it was myself and Clyde who had taken care of them, I'm not sure how she knew all that, but she did. Her first gesture was to reach up and stroke my face and she whispered to me in English, "Sam, my Warrior!" She explained this to her friends, the two Hidatsa women, and they pulled her into their arms and the three of them wept. I let them have a moment with her and went out to speak with Clyde.

Both of us knew that we had dodged a bullet that day. He had taken a knife wound in his right arm and it was already beginning to heal. He looked over my shoulders and my legs and he found that I was okay, neither of us was the worse for the wear. I asked what he had said to Astor and

Ashley and Bent. He simply said, "I told them if they didn't want more bloodshed this day, that they should make sure the four mountain men who had done this were long gone, already!" We both just stood there looking out over what was left of the rendezvous encampment.

Most of the Mountain Men would not even have known what had happened to my wife. I guess it was better that way, none of this was ever her fault anyway. But she and I would deal with it, and make sure it never happened again.

Chapter 50: Gather Up Camp

Clyde and I were sitting with our pipes outside the tent on that last day at the rendezvous while Little Fire was inside still talking to her two Hidatsa friends. We were pretty much all ready to leave the next morning but we had been discussing our options, either going down to the Arkansas River valley and our cabin there or take advantage of another cabin Bill Davis had offered us.

Just the day before, Big Bill Davis had told us of a cabin that he had built on the side of Horse Mountain in the Grand Valley region. He said we'd be welcome to it if we wanted, he was heading south toward the Arkansas, said he wanted to see Bent's new fort. That had gotten Clyde Patterson's attention right away because he said that Big Bill had been one of the builders of our cabin back there in the Gallatins where we wintered the first two years I was in the mountains. He thought if Davis were the builder, it would be a solid one.

"Been thinkin' of the Grand Valley to the south here in Colorado Territory, Mexicans pretty much giving it over to the Americans now. They say the weather there is actually splendid, not half the snow we had down on the Arkansas. We could just follow the Little Snake River south, what do you say?" Clyde asked interrupting my empty thoughts.

We had been talking with several of the mountain men about this subject. It was still early in the season, but Clyde and I had so much money that we didn't feel a need to work at our beaver trade anymore this year. We had been told by mountain men who had gone through that region called the Grand Valley, that the Utes were a friendly tribe and maintained good relations with the white settlers and mountain men.

The Grand Valley, was said had good exposure to the sun even in winter and there was very little snow because the open land of the valley gave the winter winds full free movement across the vast open space.

"You think that little gal of yours would be willing to go that far southwest? Guess it's not quite as far as the Arkansas anyway now is it?" Clyde asked addressing his thoughts out loud to me in no particular manner.

"She said she'd be willing to go wherever I go, I don't suspect that's changed much despite what just happened. She's a strong young woman and I believe she'll get over this, though it took a lot from her I'd wager. I ain't never seen her scared like that, curse them goddamn bastards!" I said to Clyde through gritted teeth.

Clyde felt some of the same feelings that I did toward her, we both would've given our lives to protect her, that's a sure thing. We sat outside the tent for a while and smoked our pipes giving the women time to talk about their issues with white men. I could hear them arguing from time to time and I rather suspect that my Little Fire was taking the side of the one white man that she knew really well, that would be me.

I knew that every year at the rendezvous there would be these kinds of attacks on native women who came with their families and their husbands to the rendezvous. It was just too hard for the men, especially the mountain men, to stay away, as the rendezvous meant so many things to those of us living in the wilds of the Rocky Mountains. Solitude did strange things to a man's mind.

After another hour I went back into the tent and sat down in silence, the women seemed pretty well talked out by now. I could see that Little Fire had regained some of her color and she seemed to be talking with the other women more freely now. When the two women left, I sat next to my wife and held her hands in mine as I looked into her eyes and tried to express how sorry I felt that this had ever happened.

We talked about the change in our plans, about going to the Grand Valley near Horse Mountain. Her response was very typical, "You have to do what you have to do, my husband. I go where you go and I do not understand men like these who can be so vicious and so demeaning. I only went to the river to get water, that's all, there was no need for them to do what they did or tried to do to me!" I could feel her tension building as she spoke of it and in some ways relived the situation she had just been through.

"There always will be men like these and we had hoped to make sure you were safe here among these rough and uncivilized men. I failed you and I apologize. I will do everything in my power so that it never happens again, ever. Clyde feels the same way as I do," I said holding her hand in both of mine.

Clyde brought some food back to the tent for the two of us that night as he began his preparations for an early morning departure the next day. Once she had eaten, Little Fire seemed to need to keep busy to keep her mind off of what had happened. She began carefully preparing our pack for the next morning, we would take down the tent before we left at dawn. It would be good to be on the road again with a new territory as our destination.

Chapter 51: Grand Valley

Once we got on the trail I could see my wife's spirits getting brighter again. It had been a very hard year for her because of the loss of so many friends and family to the smallpox epidemic in her village. Getting away from the contagion and the ominous feeling that someone close to you was going to die next, had been a real boost for her spirits. She had been looking forward to the rendezvous where she had good experiences before as a young woman.

I had to hope that sometimes these threatening situations can turn a person in a positive direction, making them more conscientious and more careful. One of the things I loved about my young wife was her carefree and fun-loving temperament. I expected that was going to change now and I wanted to be there to support her in every way I could. We were indeed partners in life now. Eventually, I wanted her to feel safe not just because of me and Clyde, but because she too could defend herself with knife, hatchet and firearms. This winter would be her time to gain these skills and this assurance.

Heading through the Little Snake River Valley as we went south gave us a view of some of the higher peaks where the lore of the mountain men said that the great dinosaurs used to roam! I never knew what to make of all of those stories, though my mother assured me that indeed these great animals had roamed the Western and parts of our country. I took her word for it but was only able to find a few mentions in some of the history books about them. No one seemed to know much about that kind of ancient history. It made me wonder what the Indian stories would tell about them.

Our first night on the trail, we went back to our routines of campfire living and it felt good. It seemed as though we had already begun to put behind us the incident at the rendezvous. I would normally have stayed up that night to smoke a pipe with my friend Clyde Patterson, but he understood I needed to go to bed early with my wife who was exhausted from the trail and needed my presence as she fell asleep.

It seems as though both of us were exhausted because I don't even remember falling asleep that night, I just remember holding her and feeling the warmth of her body and how real her commitment to me her husband, was. Several times during the night I felt her stirring and once I heard a whimper, but she didn't awaken.

I woke that next morning hearing the sounds of the coffee pot being set over the fire. When I reached out for my wife, I realized that she was already up and getting our breakfast ready. I hoped that was a good sign and I think it was. I told her that anytime she wanted to talk about what had happened I would be there to listen and support her. She smiled and went about her business that morning and we didn't speak about it for the rest of the day.

The journey to the grand Valley of the South was going to take us almost a week and a half and we enjoyed our travels on the way. We had resupplied all of our food needs and the Little Snake River Valley was abundant in game. We took a solid doe the second day out and after skinning and butchering the carcass, we had plenty of venison for a good week ahead of us. We dried some of the meat and salted it and that gave us plenty to supplement our beans and vegetables.

We had been told that there was a small settlement at Grand Junction at the southern end of the Valley and Big Bill Davis was quite effusive in his praise of the man who ran the trading post there. His name was Carlos Medina and he was part of the Mexican contingent that had staked out the Valley for the Spanish government and then for the Mexicans. The land around Grand Junction was close to Mexican territory and no one was quite sure whether it was Mexican or American, as the Mexicans didn't do much to manage such far-flung territories.

We left the Little Snake River and headed toward the mountains following a fairly bleak and desert like landscape toward the White River. We knew once we reached the White River that we would find good vegetation for the horses and also plenty of trees if we need to do for the repairs on the cabin. According to big Bill, his cabin was on the northern part of the horse mountain range, that some people were calling the White River Valley range.

We had been told that the cabin was perched on a feeder stream that descended to the Colorado River near a place called Rifle Falls. Davis wasn't quite sure, but he thought it was called the Little Elk River. That's where we were headed.

Chapter 52: Mountain Trails

The fourth night out from the rendezvous Clyde and I finally sat down and began discussing "our financials," as he called them. Between the sale of our pelts at the Collins trading post and Clyde's wagering at the rendezvous, we were a thousand dollars ahead! I really couldn't believe it when he said that. it never occurred to me that anyone could have that much money all it once. He showed me the stack of bills and the sack of gold coins that made up the entire amount.

He felt that the best way to divide the money was to split it evenly paper and gold so that each of us would have half. That had been our agreement from day one so I wasn't going to argue with him about that. He was certainly a good manager of money and he seemed to enjoy doing it. The question both of us had was whether or not we needed to do any further work this year. Clyde said that where we were headed into the White River Range of mountains we might be able to pick up a few beaver, but he knew men like Davis had mostly trapped it out.

He felt we would do much better if we hunted Wolf and Elk and possibly even some mountain goats. He said certainly those hides were much harder to come by and animals that big were harder to skin but he felt that a good bear hide was still worth a lot of money at the trading posts.

People were already beginning to talk more frequently about Buffalo hides and how important they were on the frontier. Bent's fort was shipping them by wagon all the way back to Missouri!

I told him that as far as I was concerned, taking the rest of the year off from beaver trapping would be fine with me. I had heard from the mountain men and especially from Big Bill Davis, that the weather was exceptionally warm in that region of the Rocky Mountains. Davis had said specifically that there was a lot less snow there and the summer heat was more consistent. He said it hardly ever rained and the forest were well fed by the white River in the Colorado.

That sounded like the kind of thing my wife would really enjoy, if we spent a year or two there she might even be able to put in some corn and other vegetables. As an Indian woman well-versed in the traditions of her Mandan culture, she had brought with her many sacks of seeds with the hope of planting. She never complained about our nomadic life of fur trapping. It being just the start of August, we had plenty of time for cabin building if we wanted to do so.

The cabin built by Big Bill Davis would mean that we would have almost no expenditures as far as housing went. As we picked our way through the river valley, I began to wonder whether or not I might even raise a few cattle on the land there in the grand Valley. It was well known for warm climate. I was certainly beginning to look forward to our new home and even though we had a few good rainstorms along the way, they seem to come and go quite rapidly and generally the weather was fair as we moved into the month of August and arrived finally at the banks of the White River.

The directions that Bill Davis had given us were pretty clear as long as we were sure that we were on the White River and headed south toward the Colorado. We were on our tenth day out when we came in sight of the cabin. We had followed the Little Elk River, which was just a big stream up the mountainside toward a clearing that we could just barely see through the trees. And there it was, a fine cabin! The roof had come apart a little bit and obviously would let in some rain, but it was early August and we had plenty of time to make any repairs that were needed.

Clyde and I had procured good saws and axes at the rendezvous, knowing that we would need them when it came time to do cabin repairs. Because she had grown up in a log and mud hut, Little Fire was not at all intimidated by the idea of living in a log cabin. I believe she could've made do anywhere, she was that kind of resourceful person, just by her nature.

The walls of the cabin had held pretty well and you could see where an occasional bear had tried to break into one of the windows that was covered with a wood lattice. Birds had nested in the broken roof slats, but it looked as though this cabin could be our new home for quite a while! The nice thing about it all was we had several really good months of weather to make any preparations we needed. In the meantime, Clyde would explore the surrounding valleys

and mountain ledges to see what kind of game we might
count on in this part of the wilderness.

Chapter 53: Settling In

Our cabin was situated about 2000 feet above the valley floor which probably put it somewhere in the mid six thousand foot range. It was well below the Rocky Mountain tree line and in the thick of a rich pine forest where a lot of aspens grew. It looked as though the cabin had been inhabited at least several winter seasons. I was beginning to realize that mountain men moved around throughout the Rockies, setting up a cabin here and a cabin there for their winter hibernation.

Clyde told me that he knew of at least three such cabins that Bill Davis had put up, and the big man really knew how to put together a log cabin! From the front step of our cabin we could look down over the valley and see for what seemed to be about a hundred miles on a clear day. After we had been there couple of weeks in the cabin was looking really good I told Clyde that I was going to set up a kind of a screen for our bed bedroom, for Little Fire and myself. He said he thought that was a good idea and I began quickly cutting straight thin poles to form a sort of a wall.

We would hang their skins in buffalo robes on the wall to give it more privacy and to keep some warmth in. It took less than a week to complete that little job, but it gave me an idea. "What would you say if I wanted to build a whole room, an addition onto the end of the cabin? The ledge extends far enough and the ground is stable. The river is on the other side, and I would only have to put up three walls!" I said one evening as we smoked in front of the fireplace.

There was a big fireplace to the left of the entrance and there we did most of our cooking and it kept the room of the cabin at a fairly even temperature. At night we could warm big rocks to put in our bed when the winter nights got really cold. The temperature rarely got much below freezing we were told and that too would be a blessing after the wind and cold of the Missouri Valley in Dakota territory.

Clyde liked the idea of the addition and we started pacing it off the next morning. Little Fire reminded me that among her people it was the women who built the huts, so she was even more excited than I was. By sunset that day we had already cut five good-sized logs! It took about three weeks to get the frame up for the roof. September turned out to be a warm month this year, and we found some leftover cement in the horse shed that made it possible to have a small fireplace in the "Ogden's Room," as Clyde called it.

We had the walls chinked by early October and we moved in the next week. I would spend the winter making furniture with Clyde, who loved a project like that. We had turned the old horse shed into a makeshift workshop.

To my surprise my industrious wife had planted beans on the sunny field that extended out from our cabin and soon the plants were growing very rapidly and by the end of August they were producing and we had fresh beans for our daily stew. Though she hadn't anticipated it, her little garden also brought in several curious deer which made it easy for me to harvest venison when we needed it.

The only problem with the deer population was that my wife began to be it attached to them and she was actually feeding them. That meant that when I shot one of the young deer that she had taken a fancy to, I had to go off to the deep forest and skin it out there and harvest the meat for our table. She just didn't want to know which deer it was I'd killed!

Clyde and I had quickly gotten the corral fixed up for the horses and once the cabin project was finished we used the extra time to build a lean to where they could shelter through the winter months. We also began cutting hay in some of the neighboring fields so they would have plenty of food for the winter. As usual, the wood supply was my responsibility and I welcomed the physical exercise of sawing and splitting and stacking the wood.

Little Fire and I had discovered a beautiful waterfall on the stream that flowed past our cabin. We would go off there for little picnics from time to time and it was a fun place to bathe, it felt like our little piece of paradise. Clyde and I recognize right away that there had been beaver activity here quite some time ago and that the reason the cabin was there was probably because trappers that come along and cleaned out the streams, wiping out the entire population of the area.

We would have to go pretty far afield if we wanted to do any beaver trapping in that area! But Clyde assured me that he would find out what the possibilities were after he made his first trip down to Grand Junction. We knew about the town at the lake and at the confluence of the waters there was called Grand Junction. There was a Mexican trading post and Clyde was eager to check it out. I think the money that he had in his pocket was burning a hole there and he needed to spend some money, but I encouraged him to make the journey on his own since it was only one overnight.

I was quite amazed at how strange it felt to have Little Fire all to myself there in the cabin and we took advantage of our time alone I can tell you that! In fact, I think we may have our first child to thank for that little vacation that Clyde took down at Grand Junction.

About the Author

Robert M Johnson has spent a good portion of his adult life living in mountain regions. He currently lives in Virginia just fifty miles from where John Coulter, the great frontiersman was born. The life of frontiersmen like Sam Ogden is a constant struggle with the elements, the changes in seasons, altitude, animal migrations, and human greed.

The author has spent countless hours hiking and camping in high mountain regions. His interest in all things western has been a lifelong passion. The period between 1810 and 1860 holds a special place for him. The information and inspiration that we have from this historical time in the American West is certainly a rich source of ideas and ideals.

In this fifth volume of the Sam Ogden Series, a winter with the Mandan Indians had to be cut short because of a smallpox epidemic that ravaged the Slanted Village. The Missouri River had become a place of white man's commerce, bringing with it some of the white man's diseases. Sam left the village with his Mandan Wife and his partner Clyde Patterson to do some beaver trapping in the Rocky Mountains.

Made in the USA
Middletown, DE
24 September 2022

11151722R00106